SHIPMENT 1

Cowboy Sanctuary by Elle James
Dade by Delores Fossen
Finding a Family by Judy Christenberry
The Family Plan by Cathy McDavid
Daddy's Double Duty by Stella Bagwell
The Sheriff's Son by Barbara White Daille

SHIPMENT 2

A Bride for a Blue-Ribbon Cowboy by Judy Duarte
A Family for the Rugged Rancher by Donna Alward
The Doctor Wore Boots by Debra Webb
A Cowboy's Redemption by Jeannie Watt
Marrying Molly by Christine Rimmer
Frisco Joe's Fiancée by Tina Leonard

SHIPMENT 3

Dancing in the Moonlight by RaeAnne Thayne
One Tough Cowboy by Sara Orwig
The Rancher's Runaway Princess by Donna Alward
A Taste of Paradise by Patricia Thayer
Her Cowboy Daddy by Cathy Gillen Thacker
Cattleman's Honor by Pamela Toth
The Texan's Secret by Linda Warren

SHIPMENT 4

Fannin's Flame by Tina Leonard
Texas Cinderella by Victoria Pade
Maddie Inherits a Cowboy by Jeannie Watt
The Wrangler by Pamela Britton
The Reluctant Wrangler by Roxann Delaney
Rachel's Cowboy by Judy Christenberry

SHIPMENT 5

Rodeo Daddy by Marin Thomas
His Medicine Woman by Stella Bagwell
A Real Live Cowboy by Judy Duarte
Wyatt's Ready-Made Family by Patricia Thayer
The Cowboy Code by Christine Wenger
A Rancher's Pride by Barbara White Daille

SHIPMENT 6

Cowboy Be Mine by Tina Leonard
Big Sky Bride, Be Mine! by Victoria Pade
Hard Case Cowboy by Nina Bruhns
Texas Heir by Linda Warren
Bachelor Cowboy by Roxann Delaney
The Forgotten Cowboy by Kara Lennox
The Prodigal Texan by Lynnette Kent

SHIPMENT 7

The Bull Rider's Secret by Marin Thomas
Lone Star Daddy by Stella Bagwell
The Cowboy and the Princess by Myrna Mackenzie
Dylan's Last Dare by Patricia Thayer
Made for a Texas Marriage by Crystal Green
Cinderella and the Cowboy by Judy Christenberry

SHIPMENT 8

Samantha's Cowboy by Marin Thomas
Cowboy at the Crossroads by Linda Warren
Rancher and Protector by Judy Christenberry
Texas Trouble by Kathleen O'Brien
Vegas Two-Step by Liz Talley
A Cowgirl's Secret by Laura Marie Altom

Texas Heir

LINDA WARREN

◆ **HARLEQUIN**® WESTERN PROMISES

If you purchased this book without a cover you should be aware
that this book is stolen property. It was reported as "unsold and
destroyed" to the publisher, and neither the author nor the
publisher has received any payment for this "stripped book."

Recycling programs
for this product may
not exist in your area.

ISBN-13: 978-0-373-00357-0

Texas Heir

Copyright © 2008 by Linda Warren

All rights reserved. Except for use in any review, the reproduction or
utilization of this work in whole or in part in any form by any electronic,
mechanical or other means, now known or hereinafter invented, including
xerography, photocopying and recording, or in any information storage
or retrieval system, is forbidden without the written permission of the
publisher, Harlequin Enterprises Limited, 225 Duncan Mill Road,
Don Mills, Ontario M3B 3K9, Canada.

This is a work of fiction. Names, characters, places and incidents are
either the product of the author's imagination or are used fictitiously,
and any resemblance to actual persons, living or dead, business
establishments, events or locales is entirely coincidental.

This edition published by arrangement with Harlequin Books S.A.

For questions and comments about the quality of this book,
please contact us at CustomerService@Harlequin.com.

® and TM are trademarks of Harlequin Enterprises Limited or its
corporate affiliates. Trademarks indicated with ® are registered in the
United States Patent and Trademark Office, the Canadian Intellectual
Property Office and in other countries.

Printed in U.S.A.

Two-time RITA® Award–nominated and award-winning author **Linda Warren** loves her job, writing happily-ever-after books for Harlequin. Drawing upon her years of growing up on a farm/ranch in Texas, she writes with an emotional punch about sexy heroes, feisty heroines and broken families, all set against the backdrop of Texas. Her favorite pastime is sitting on her patio with her husband watching the wildlife. Learn more about Linda and her books at her website, lindawarren.net, or on Facebook, LindaWarrenAuthor, or follow @Texauthor on Twitter.

Books by Linda Warren

Harlequin American Romance

The Christmas Cradle
Christmas, Texas Style
The Cowboy's Return
Once a Cowboy
Texas Heir
The Sheriff of Horseshoe, Texas
Her Christmas Hero
Tomas: Cowboy Homecoming
One Night in Texas
A Texas Holiday Miracle

Texas Rebels

Texas Rebels: Egan
Texas Rebels: Falcon

Visit the Author Profile page at Harlequin.com for more titles.

A special thanks to Gary Simmons
for being so generous in sharing his knowledge of
private jets and aircraft. And to Sara Schroeder for
sharing her visit to west Texas. Also, to Jane Pearce
for graciously giving me a Spanish lesson.

And last, to Pam Litton, Lee Dewbre,
Linda Stewart, Linda Hermes and
Colleen Thompson for offering help when
I needed it the most. All errors are strictly mine.

Chapter One

Cari Michaels was having a "take two Tylenol" type of day.

And it was only five minutes to eight.

With tires squealing, she swerved into her parking spot with the speed and arrogance of her sixteen-year-old nephew. She had five minutes to make the executive meeting on time.

Why was Reed Dalton Preston, CEO of Dalton's Department Stores, calling an impromptu gathering of his executives this early? The one morning her alarm clock chose to die.

Seconds ticked away.

No sweat. She'd make it.

Thrusting the gearshift into Park, she turned off the engine and grabbed her purse and briefcase. Then she was off at a run for the elevator, her heels tapping in three-quarter time across the pavement in the parking garage. She prayed Homer, the elevator operator, was waiting with the door open.

He was. She could see his smiling round face, and then she heard a snap. The next thing she knew she was kissing hard, dirty concrete. She moaned as burning needles of pain shot through her knee and elbow.

Damn! Damn! Damn!

Her day just got worse.

"Ms. Cari, are you okay?" Through a wave of humiliation she heard Homer's worried voice and rolled to her feet faster than a quarterback nailed for a loss.

"Yes, Homer. I'm fine." She brushed off her black Prada pantsuit and took a deep breath. "Just broke a heel." She raised her foot to remove the offending shoe and held it up, but she didn't have a moment to chat. Time was running out and she knew she'd get "The Look" from Reed if she slid into her seat one second late.

Homer picked up her briefcase and purse

and handed them to her with a concerned look in his eyes.

"Thank you," she said, and hobbled into the elevator. "Can you make Louise fly?"

"No, ma'am," Homer replied, adjusting his bellman's cap with the Dalton logo on it. "She only goes one speed." Homer was mentally challenged and he took his job seriously. He'd named the elevator Louise and sometimes he stayed until every executive was out of the building because he didn't like anyone pushing Louise's buttons but him. Everyone loved Homer, including Cari.

As the elevator smoothly glided upward she removed her other heel. Being just five feet three inches tall, she really needed the heels for the extra confidence-boosting height.

Glancing down, she saw she'd ripped her slacks at the knee. There was also dirt on her cobalt-blue silk blouse. Great. Now she was going to look like a street urchin, but she wasn't missing the meeting.

Elevator music, Bach or Beethoven or something, played in the background and it started to get on her nerves. Why was this thing going so slow? Louise needed a checkup.

"My mama says it doesn't matter what you

look like as long as you have a good heart." Homer's bit of wisdom made Cari wonder if she looked that bad.

"You have a good heart, Ms. Cari."

"Thank you, Homer. So do you."

The doors opened. She smiled at Homer a second before she dashed out and down the hall to the private door of her office.

Homer's "Have a good day" followed her.

She threw the shoes and her briefcase onto her desk and took a moment to glance at herself in the mirror by the door. Slipping her purse strap over her shoulder, she ran her fingers through her short, blow-and-go, dark brown hair. At the moment it was more blow than go.

Her sister, the beautician, had talked her into the style. Chic and stylish, Kitty had said—just what Cari needed for her busy lifestyle. Shaking her head, she hoped her hair looked chic instead of looking more like it had been cut with a weed-eater.

And who's going to notice, she asked herself as she darted out the door to the boardroom. Certainly not Reed Preston. Cari remembered vividly the first time she had seen Reed. He and Richard Preston, his father, were making a tour of the store, something Mr. Preston didn't do too often. But Reed was home for the summer from the University of Texas and Mr. Preston was priming him to take over the reins of Dalton's. Everyone had been on their toes, watching their p's and q's for the momentous occasion.

She'd been a naive, gauche teenager determined to make something of her life away from the small farm where she'd been raised. When she looked at Reed, she saw everything she'd been looking for and everything she could never have. He was tall with dark hair and warm, brown eyes. Cari knew Reed was as far out of her reach as Prince William. Not that she wanted the prince, but that's how she thought of Reed—as the Prince of Dalton's.

So did a lot of other women.

She kept her feelings secret. No one knew how she felt about Reed except Marisa Kincaid, Reed's sister, a woman whose struggles with her difficult, demanding family had put her in desperate need of a good friend.

When Marisa was seventeen she'd fallen in love with a rodeo cowboy, Colter Kincaid. Marisa was in training to be a concert pianist and her involvement with Colter was unacceptable to the Prestons. With lies and threats her family had broken them up, but Marisa soon discovered she was pregnant. Unable to locate Colter, Marisa had to deal with her parents alone. She refused abortion and adoption, intending to keep her baby. She had underestimated her parents, though.

Marisa had problems with the pregnancy, so the Prestons devised a plan. They told their daughter the baby was stillborn. In truth, they had called Colter and offered him the baby. For years Marisa grieved for her child. At the time she lived with her mother in New York, and she sank into deep depression, unable to play the piano. Her father had brought her to Texas to heal.

Once Marisa was in Texas, the lies and deceit began to unravel. Marisa found out her daughter was very much alive. It had taken a while, but she and Colter had fallen in love again, too. It hadn't been an easy time and Cari had been there for Marisa when she'd needed to talk. Cari admitted their friendship had undoubtedly helped her gain a vice presidency at Dalton's, but she also had earned it.

She had realized at an early age that she didn't want to spend the rest of her life as a salesclerk and, with four siblings, her parents couldn't afford to send her to college or even junior college. So that first year she'd saved every dime she could and took night courses at a junior college, finally finishing up her business degree at the University of Texas in Dallas while continuing to work for Dalton's.

When she entered the boardroom, Cari summoned her years of experience and quietly took her seat at the polished oak table, which could seat twenty people. The paneling on the walls was made of the same vibrant wood, trimmed in an ornate, hand-carved pattern unlike anything Cari had ever seen. Photos of all the stores across Texas, as well as the store's founder, Harold Dalton, hung on the walls. The first time Cari had stepped into this room the sight of it had taken her breath away.

An arrangement of white irises and lavender lilacs took pride of place in the center of the table. Fresh flowers always adorned this room. Their delicate fragrance drifted to her and Cari relaxed, uncaring that her slacks were torn and her blouse was dirty.

The executive team had already taken their seats and Reed stood at the head of the table, looking directly at her. She stared back at him. Yet those honey brown eyes didn't waver for a second.

Nor did hers.

"Nice of you to join us, Ms. Michaels," he said in his deep, smooth voice that usually curled her toes into her shoes. Since she wasn't wearing shoes, her toes curled against the polished hardwood floor that felt cool to her stocking feet.

She smiled sweetly, not rising to the bait.

"I know you're wondering why I called this meeting." Reed turned his attention elsewhere and she let out her breath, not even realizing she was holding it. Her elbow was throbbing and she just wanted to go to her office and regroup for the day. She was sure she'd left her pride somewhere on that garage floor and she desperately needed to get it back.

George, the man on her right, sat with a pen in his hand ready to jot down every word out of Reed's mouth. Mike, across from her, was poised the same way. Cari's pen was in her purse and she didn't see the need to fish for it. Reed's personal assistant always sent memos just in case anyone missed anything.

"I'll make this short," Reed said. "I know you're eager to get back to your jobs. Or at least I hope you are."

That caused a round of muffled laughter.

Cari took a moment to study Reed. In jeans, a crisp white shirt, a lightweight sports jacket and cowboy boots—she couldn't see them but she knew he always wore custom-made Kincaid boots—he appeared to have stepped out of the pages of *Texas Monthly* magazine. His tall lean frame showed off the clothes, but there was something about him that bespoke power and wealth. Maybe it was the way he looked directly into your eyes. Or that strong chin. Or that razzle-dazzle, made-for-Hollywood smile. Or an elusive quality that was embedded in the way he moved and spoke.

But to her it was none of those things. She admired the man within, the man who was striving to prove to his father he could run Dalton's with strength and compassion. Reed was more involved with his employees than Mr. Preston had ever been. Homer had a job because of Reed. Mr. Preston would never have allowed Homer to be hired.

Reed had new ideas and a new way of doing business. It was showing results. Profits were at an all-time high and Cari enjoyed working with her boss, being on his team. But she wondered if he'd ever see her as a woman.

A desirable woman.

At thirty-four, marriage and family were becoming important to her. If she kept waiting for Reed Preston, her biological clock was going to spit and sputter and run out of time.

"I wanted to let my executive team know before the news hits the papers," Reed was saying. "Daphne Harwood and I are engaged. We're planning an early spring wedding."

What did he say?

People jumped up, shaking his hand and congratulating him. Cari felt herself turning to stone. All her dreams, everything she'd ever hoped for, ended in that moment. Somewhere within her she found the strength to get to her feet. She had to. She was a professional.

Without shoes.

Was there something symbolic in that? What could it be? If Reed had a glass slipper, she definitely had a foot to put in it. A bubble of hysterical laughter rose in her throat and she immediately pushed it down.

"I would like for you to meet her. She's waiting in my office." He pushed a button on the phone to his left and then glanced at them. "Please make her feel welcome." Reed motioned to someone at the door and a goddess walked in. That was the only way to describe Reed's fiancée, Daphne. Tall, with champagne-blond hair and gorgeous blue eyes, Daphne's body was a perfect ten on anyone's scale.

Even Cari's.

Where in the hell did she come from? Marisa hadn't mentioned Reed was dating anyone special. Reed's dating life was a revolving door of beautiful women. No one had told her the door had stopped revolving. When did this happen?

Reed was introducing Daphne to each person and explaining their job. Oh great! She stood on her tiptoes, not that that was going to help her height a lot. Why did she have to break her damn heel?

There wasn't enough Tylenol in the world to fix this day.

Or her broken heart.

She braced herself as they approached.

"This is Cari Michaels, vice president," Reed said. "She's basically my right hand. I can always depend on Cari to—" he noticed her shoeless feet and torn slacks "—what happened?"

"Nothing." She brushed his concern away. "I took a tumble in the garage and broke a heel, that's all."

"Maybe you should see a doctor," Daphne

said in a silky voice that managed to rub against Cari's nerves like coarse burlap.

"Yes," Reed said. "That's a good idea."

"No." Cari felt dwarfed and insignificant by the tall goddess and Reed standing side by side. They reminded her of a model bride and groom atop a wedding cake. "I'm fine, really." She held out her hand. As their palms touched, she noted Daphne's fingers were soft, fragile almost, but that's not what held Cari's attention. It was the large diamond sparkling on her left hand. "It's nice to meet you and I wish you both the very best."

She moved away as quickly as possible, her words ringing in her ears. She prayed they'd sounded normal. She could be a sore loser if she had ever been in the game, but she had never even walked onto the field.

Only in her dreams.

"Cari." Reed caught up with her at the door. "Our plane leaves at one. Will you be ready? We can postpone the trip if you're not up to it."

Good heavens, the morning's events had caused the scheduled September trip to the El Paso store to slip her mind. Her overnight bag was in her car, so her amnesia was only temporary. Reed made random visits to all the stores. He kept an up-close-and-personal connection with every store manager. They were all eager to please him.

He'd said she was his right hand and she supposed that was true. She made the trips with him and together with the manager they went over every minute detail for improvement. This was a system implemented by Reed. Richard Preston rarely visited his stores unless it was an emergency, such as a store not showing a profit.

She usually enjoyed the trips, but this one suddenly took on a feeling of gloom and doom. Spending two hours with Reed in a plane would be pure torture.

He was marrying someone else.

A painful knot clenched her stomach. The fall was the excuse she needed to avoid the trip and she was going to use it.

Coward.

The word ran through her system like the cheap moonshine she and her cousins had gotten drunk on as teenagers. It had made her sick then and she felt sick now.

But she'd never taken the easy way out and she wasn't about to start.

"I'm fine and I'll be ready."

With as much dignity as possible, she walked out of the room.

Reed stared after her. Cari looked upset and he wondered why. She couldn't be upset about the engagement, could she? It was probably just her fall. He should cancel the trip, yet Cari would have a fit if he treated her with kid gloves. She was direct and honest and he had to take her at her word.

His sister, Marisa, had really hoped he and Cari would become a couple, but they had never made that connection. Cari was a bundle of energy, determined to succeed in the business world. With sheer grit and guts, she had climbed the corporate ladder at Dalton's.

Her confidence and drive sometimes threw him. He was used to women fawning over him and going out of their way to please him. Cari had done none of those things. She taunted him by calling him Junior and her dark eyes dared him to reprimand her, which he often did.

They had that type of relationship, vocal and explosive. Sparks always seemed to fly when they were together. It was a great working relationship. That was the most important thing to both of them.

The situation had changed somewhat last Fourth of July and he still cursed himself for his momentary lapse. Marisa and her husband, Colter, had thrown a big party at their ranch and Cari and Reed were invited along with a lot of their friends. Everyone else there was part of a couple, so they were paired together. The evening had been fun, with a lot of laughing and ribbing. In the backyard they popped fireworks and watched the glittering sparks light up the sky.

Standing in the moonlight, Cari had smiled at him and without thinking he'd kissed her. It lasted a mind-blowing split second before he realized what he was doing and pulled away. Cari had never shown a romantic interest in him. Her career was her life. She gave Dalton's one hundred percent of herself and he wasn't jeopardizing that. They had a business relationship. Period.

In a rush he'd said, "Happy Fourth of July."

She'd smiled and wished him the same.

Her reaction was a relief. No way was he dating a woman who worked for him even if his sister wanted him to. He steered clear of setups. His parents were constantly trying to fix him up with the perfect woman. Their attention to his marital status made him feel pressured and restless. It was important to him that he make his own choices, especially in women.

At times, though, he wondered what would have happened if he hadn't stopped kissing Cari.

"Darling." Daphne laid a hand on his arm. "Is everything okay?"

He looked into her beautiful eyes and was so grateful he'd finally found the woman for him. It had been a whirlwind courtship and at the end of four weeks he'd proposed.

Marriage had never been on his list of top priorities. His parents had a marriage from hell and his friends were all playing marriage roulette. He had to admit that Marisa and Colter were happy, and as he grew older he realized he wanted that—to find the perfect woman, if there was such a person, to share his life and to raise a family together.

His parents had manipulated him and Marisa all their lives and the last thing Reed needed was a woman his parents had picked for him. Ironically a business acquaintance of his dad's had been invited for dinner and his daughter was in town. His mother was a fanatic about her dinner parties and the proper seating. She'd begged Reed to attend so the young woman wouldn't feel out of place.

To his surprise he and Daphne had hit it off from the start. She was independently wealthy, so she wasn't after him for his money. She was a ballet dancer and had just returned from touring France. That threw him at first because his mother had been a dancer, but Daphne was different. She donated a lot of her time to children's charities and put on special shows to entertain many of them. He admired everything about her. Also, she wanted a home and family like he did. They were perfect for each other.

The date hadn't been a setup. His parents hadn't even known Mr. Harwood's daughter was in town until the last minute. So it was a nice surprise for all of them.

"Yes." He kissed her cheek. "Everything is fine."

For some reason though he couldn't stop himself from staring at the doorway where Cari had stood.

Cari rushed through her secretary's office to reach her own, not bothering to go through her private entrance. "Get me a tall mocha frappuccino with an extra shot of espresso, please," she said to Heather.

"Yes, ma'am." Heather was instantly on her feet.

"I already have it."

Cari whirled around to see Marisa standing there with two coffees. She quickly reached for one. "I knew I loved you for a reason." She took a sip and glanced at Heather, who was staring at her with wide eyes. At twenty-four she looked like a teenager. Cari knew she must have looked the same years ago.

"Please get me the itinerary for the El Paso trip."

"Yes, ma'am."

Marisa followed her into her office. "I see you've heard the news."

Cari took a big swallow of coffee. "If you mean about Reed and the debutante, yes, I just heard."

"I'm sorry. I tried calling but you didn't answer."

"Oh." Cari patted her pockets with one hand. "I'm not sure where my cell is. I guess I left it at home."

Marisa gave Cari's disheveled appearance the once-over. "What happened?"

"Don't ask."

"Okay," Marisa said slowly, watching her. "I tried to get here earlier, but it's a mad rush to get the kids off to school, and this morning Ellie was having a fit about her hair. Since she's become a teenager, the naturally curly hair has become more of an issue. We seem to spend every morning taming it."

"No big deal," Cari replied with a wave of her hand.

She could feel Marisa's eyes on her. "I know how you feel about Reed."

Her eyes flew to meet her friend's. "That's just between you and me." With a sigh, she sank into her chair and took another gulp of coffee. Setting the paper cup on her desk, she asked, "Where did she come from? Has he been dating her long?"

Marisa sat in a rose chintz chair, placing her purse on the floor. "My parents hosted a dinner for them last night and Colter and I met her for the first time. She's a daughter of a business acquaintance of my dad's."

"You're kidding." Cari sat up straighter. "I would have thought Reed would have avoided her like toxic waste."

It was a well-known fact that Richard and Vanessa Preston had ideas about who Reed should marry—someone with their social standing and assets. But since the fiasco with Marisa, Reed ignored his parents and chose his own women.

"Me, too." Marisa crossed her legs and took a sip of her coffee. "I think it was love at first sight. One of those wham-bam things."

"Mmm." Cari twisted her cup, feeling the warmth against her thumb. She thought that strange when she felt so cold inside.

"Cari, I'm sorry."

Cari looked into her friend's honey-warm eyes and saw all her concern and caring. Marisa was one of those women who was beautiful on the outside as well as within. Looking at her delicate features and curly hair, one would think she was fragile and weak, but Marisa was one of the strongest women she knew.

"Hey, don't feel sorry for me," she told her. "Reed and I weren't meant to be together. We've had a number of years to connect and we haven't."

Marisa glanced at her over the rim of her coffee cup. "I wonder why?"

"Incompatible," Cari joked.

"But you work so well together."

They did, but Cari didn't know how much longer she could continue to do that.

"We don't let our personal feelings get in the way of business. Dalton's is always our top priority."

Marisa looked straight at her. "You care more about Dalton's than I ever did."

"When you have to earn something, it means so much more."

"I think that's it."

Cari blinked. "What? What are you talking about?"

"Reed and I were born with the proverbial silver spoon in our mouths. By birth, everything was given to us. We earned nothing, but you've had to fight your way up. The first thing I noticed about you was your determination and confidence."

"So?"

"I never think of you as being afraid, but I think you're afraid of my parents and their social status and expectations. You're afraid you won't fit in or live up to their ideal mate for Reed. In your mind, you're still that farm girl from Hillsboro, Texas."

"That's—"

"It's true." Marisa didn't give her a chance to voice a protest. "If you had gone after Reed, you would have been a couple a long time ago."

Cari bit her lip, not bothering to lie to her friend. "Your mother ties my nerves into tight knots, and after a meeting with your father I have to rush to my office and put my head between my legs to catch my breath again. I don't know why I'm always trying to fit in."

Marisa got up and came around the desk. Sitting on the edge, she placed her cup behind her. "Why do you have to try at all? You're an intelligent, kind, beautiful, funny and compassionate woman. I'm lucky to have you for a friend and I'm so grateful you're in my life. Just be yourself. My parents are just people and sometimes they haven't been very kind or understanding. So don't ever think you're less than them."

"You don't know what it's like to be raised poor and to never have anything. People look down on you and that's hard to overcome." Suddenly Cari remembered the homemade hand-me-down clothes, food stamps and welfare. Her past was like a scar on her soul that would never heal.

"Cari Michaels, I'm going to shake you. Look at all you've accomplished. From a saleswoman you've risen to a high-paying position in a billion-dollar corporation. That's no small feat."

Cari lifted an eyebrow. "It helps to have friends in high places."

"Who?"

"You, of course."

Marisa frowned. "I had nothing to do with you getting this job."

"When you left, you suggested—"

"No, I didn't," Marisa quickly interrupted. "I was busy planning a wedding and getting to know my daughter. Dad and Reed always fill the top positions. Your job performance was miles above the rest. I'm sure there was never any doubt about moving you up. My father's not an idiot. He knows who's best for Dalton's."

Cari was stunned. She'd thought Marisa had gotten her the position. Suddenly she was feeling so many things and each one was labeled stupid with a capital S. Confidence was always her strong suit...yet at times it was her weakest.

"Okay." She ruffled her hair with her hands. "I'll admit I have a problem in that area, but I really thought you put in a word for me."

"Please." Marisa slid off the desk. "You don't need a word from me. Everything you've accomplished you've done on your own. You can stand toe-to-toe with my parents and Reed. I don't understand why you get so down on yourself at times."

"I guess I love the misery."

Marisa pointed a finger at her. "Repeat after me—I am terrific. I am a woman and there's not one damn thing I can't do. Even recover from a broken heart."

Cari smiled and stood, hugging her friend. "Thanks. I needed that today."

"We have to find you a boyfriend," Marisa said, her eyes twinkling. "My rodeo husband knows a lot of cowboys. How would you like to date a cowboy?"

Her smile broadened. "I saw on a billboard somewhere 'Save a horse, ride a cowboy,' so I'm game. If you find a good-looking cowboy in tight jeans who doesn't chew tobacco, I'll go out with him. I'll put a hitch in his giddyup and a grin on my face."

They burst out laughing and Cari felt a whole lot better.

Marisa sobered. "You have to come for dinner tonight. The kids would love to see you and we can ply Colter for viable candidates."

"Why didn't you think of me when Tripp and Brodie were available?" They were Colter's incredibly handsome best friends who were now happily married.

"Because you were hung up on you know who."

"Not anymore."

After a long pause, Marisa asked, "Are you sure?"

"Yes," she replied, but she hesitated. She hated herself for that.

"If you're not, this is the time to let Reed know how you feel."

Cari gasped. "Marisa Kincaid, I can't believe you said that."

Marisa walked around the desk and reached for her purse on the floor. "I just don't want you or Reed to make a mistake."

"Don't you like Daphne?"

Marisa brushed back her blond curls and appeared thoughtful for a minute. "Daphne is who I would be if I had continued living with my mother in New York, adhering to the strict regimen she had planned for me. Daphne is structured, disciplined and perfect, but in the two hours I spent with her last night I never heard her laugh. That bothered me."

"Why?"

"I never laughed until I met Colter. He opened doors to emotions I didn't know existed and I know with all my heart that a person has to laugh to be really happy."

"Maybe she was just nervous." Cari didn't understand why she was defending the blond beauty. "Meeting your parents can be traumatic for anyone."

"She'd already met them."

"Okay. Daphne doesn't laugh, but Reed loves her."

Marisa shrugged. "I'm being catty and that's all I'm saying. What time do you want to come out for dinner?"

"Oh, I'm sorry. We're flying to the El Paso store today."

"We? As in you and Reed?"

"Yes."

"Mmm." Cari could almost see the plans tripping through Marisa's head, but she didn't voice them. "We'll do it when you get back then."

"Sure."

Marisa paused and looked into Cari's eyes. "Remember what I said."

"Marisa—"

Marisa held up a hand, stopping her. "This is your last chance."

Cari knew her friend had good intentions, but Marisa didn't know everything.

Marisa stared at Cari's heels on the top of her desk. "I'm not even going to ask what your shoes are doing on your desk or why one heel is broken. The less I know the better. Call me when you get back."

"I didn't use it as a weapon if that's what you're thinking," Cari called to her retreating back.

Or on your brother's head.

Chapter Two

Cari sank into her chair, rubbing her throbbing elbow, her thoughts wandering into treacherous territory. She and Marisa shared a lot, but there was one thing she hadn't shared. It had happened on the Fourth of July and Cari was still struggling to understand it herself.

Marisa and Colter had thrown a big barbecue for all their friends. Everyone laughed and visited and had a great time. In the evening Colter had a fireworks display for the kids.

Colter had a couple of water hoses hooked up in case sparks caused a fire. Jack thought the hoses were for fun and started squirting the kids and then letting the hose run all over him. Colter quickly had his son under control and Marisa had taken Jack into the house to change his clothes. She and Reed were laughing at Jack's silly antics, and then suddenly he was looking into her eyes in a way he never had before. It wasn't businesslike.

The moonlight was intoxicating and everyone else faded away. Reed had bent his head and gently kissed her lips. It had been exciting, exhilarating and everything she'd ever imagined. For a moment she'd returned the kiss with years of pent-up yearnings.

In the split second it had taken those feelings to take hold, it had taken half that for him to pull away. Suddenly a wall of fear and insecurity blindsided her. He'd never kissed her before. From his "Happy Fourth of July" she knew it was only a friendly gesture. Had she made a fool of herself?

She'd said something and she couldn't even remember what. Reed left soon after. From then on, their relationship had changed. It was all business now. They didn't joke around the way they used to and she didn't call him Junior anymore.

In the past two months she'd wanted to

talk about the kiss, but she could never get up enough nerve to even broach the subject. She'd hoped and prayed he'd bring it up, but he hadn't.

When the kiss had ended abruptly, she had been both disappointed and relieved. She still wasn't sure what the relief was really about. Was she afraid if he continued with the kiss she would reveal her true feelings? Would Reed tell her he could never become involved with someone who wasn't in his circle of accepted friends?

At her age it seemed almost impossible that she would allow herself to believe such a thing. She was Marisa's best friend and the Prestons had accepted her as such. Mainly because they knew Marisa wouldn't allow anything else.

Reed had those same ethics. Her roots and blue-collar family would make no difference to him.

So why was she so afraid to take a chance? Why was she so afraid to confront Reed about her feelings?

She knew it had something to do with the razzle-dazzle shine of Richard Reed Dalton Preston. Was she happier living with the fantasy of her Prince Charming? Without his shine he'd become just a man. Maybe she was afraid of what that would reveal.

About him.

But mostly about herself.

Perhaps she was one of those women who were only attracted to the shine. Inside her, a sprout of fear took root. Razzle-dazzle shine didn't last forever and she didn't have the courage to find out what happened afterward. That said she was shallow and weak.

Or she was good at protecting her heart. She never wanted to feel that kind of pain again—the pain of not being good enough.

She picked up the broken high heel from her desk. As little girls, she and her sisters loved the story of Cinderella and dreamed of a fancy shoe they could slip on their foot to magically change their whole lives—away from the farm with a handsome prince.

But she wasn't a little girl anymore. She was a grown woman and knew that fairy tales only existed in little girls' dreams.

She also knew something else. No one was ever again going to make her feel less than she was.

Not the Prestons.

And certainly not Reed.

Cari studied the shoe for an extra moment

and wondered if she had the courage to express her feelings and wait for Reed's reaction. Reed had found the woman for him and that was it. Game. Set. Match. So it was over. Her feelings were inconsequential.

But what if Daphne wasn't right for him?

Cari closed her eyes briefly, hearing Marisa's words.

This is your last chance.

Suddenly she realized the truth of those words. It was now or never. They would have time to talk on the plane. She knew his moods. If he was happy, then she wouldn't say a word about her feelings. If she sensed any doubts then she would open up and ask if he had ever thought of her in a romantic way.

She would bring up the kiss. That could unlock a whole new realm of heartache, but she wasn't going to let him slip away without saying something.

Think about your job, echoed through her head. Her job gave her prestige, status and an identity. She was Cari Michaels, vice president of Dalton's Department Stores. People looked up to her, valued her opinions. Could she risk losing that? Could she risk losing everything that made her feel strong and worthy?

With a sigh, she pushed the button for Heather, who breezed through the door immediately and laid the El Paso itinerary in front of her.

"Thanks." Cari held up the heels, her mind shifting to business. "Put these in a plastic bag and carry them to George Ortell, please. I want to know who supplies these shoes to Dalton's and I want an explanation of why this heel broke so easily."

She could look up the information herself, but George had taken over dealing with the suppliers and she wanted him to be on top of things. Inferior products were not carried by Dalton's.

"Okay." Heather picked up the shoes and broken heel. "In case he asks, how did the heel break?"

"I was running to make a meeting and ended up flat on my face in the parking garage."

A light dawned in Heather's eyes. "Oh. That's why you don't have on any shoes."

"Yes." Cari stared at the girl, a little puzzled at her reaction. "What did you think happened?"

Heather shrugged. "I don't know. I thought

you were making a fashion statement or something. I tell all my friends I have the coolest boss. She stands up to anyone, even Mr. Reed Preston. How many women would go to a meeting without their shoes? You're so cool."

Cari was taken aback at the praise. Heather thought she was cool. If she only knew. "Thank you, Heather." She rose to her feet. "I'm going downstairs to buy a new outfit and shoes." She could have easily had the items brought to her, but she enjoyed connecting with the sales staff.

"I'll get these to Mr. Ortell."

Cari took the regular elevator, not Homer's private executive one, to the first floor, which housed the women's and children's departments. The second floor was men's and housewares. Department-personnel offices were located on the third floor, and on the fourth floor were the executive offices. The fifth floor was a private apartment for the Preston family. It was Reed's domain—Cari had never stepped foot there.

Nor was she ever likely to now.

Within minutes she had new shoes and a new outfit and was back in the professional mode she'd mastered over the years.

* * *

George was waiting for her in her office, as she knew he would be, to talk about the defective shoe. When she and Reed returned from El Paso, they'd have a meeting to discuss whether or not Dalton's would continue to buy from that designer's company.

After George left, her mother called.

"I just wanted to remind you about Daddy's party on Sunday," Ruth Michaels said.

Cari squeezed her eyes tight. She'd forgotten. Damn! "Oh."

"It's his sixtieth birthday, Cari. Please don't miss it. It won't be the same unless all our kids are here."

Guilt weighed heavily in her chest. It was hard to find time for visits home. Her job was time consuming, with a lot of weekends spent working or traveling. Her parents didn't understand her drive for success. They wanted her to come home more often, to be a part of the family, but she was finding that harder and harder to do.

"I know I've been busy, Mama, but I won't miss Daddy's special day."

"Good. That would make him happy."

Cari hung up resolving not to miss the birthday. She'd missed too many.

* * *

Reed went over last-minute details with his personal assistant, Monica Welsby. Monica was the most organized, structured person he knew. Between her and his secretary, Adele, they kept him on top of everything. And if they just happened to miss something, he could depend on Cari to catch it. She was his safety net.

Twisting his pen, he studied his initials engraved on its gold surface, a gift from his father. Monica rattled on about the flight and visit in El Paso and her words sailed over his head. He couldn't get Cari's expression out of his mind. She was good at hiding her emotions, but he sensed she was upset about his engagement.

Why? Maybe he should have told her before the meeting, but the only people they had told were their families. With Cari's ties to Marisa she did seem like family, though.

He threw the pen onto the papers Monica had placed in front of him. He wasn't second-guessing himself over Cari. For two people who worked so well together, she had a way of getting under his skin even when she wasn't in the room.

"Is something wrong?" Monica pushed her glasses up the bridge of her nose.

"No," Reed replied and rose to his feet, feeling restless.

"Well." Monica glanced from his face to the Palm Pilot in her hand. "The limo will arrive at twelve-fifteen."

"Be sure and let Cari know."

"I've already informed Heather. Would you like me to personally call Cari?"

"No. That's fine. I just don't want any delays."

"I'm in charge, so there won't be," Monica said with an arched eyebrow, and then headed for the door.

Before Reed could gather his thoughts, Richard Preston strolled in. "Morning, son."

"Morning, Father?" he replied, taken aback by his dad's sudden appearance. His father was still chairman of the board, but he stayed out of the daily business of running Dalton's. That was the only way Reed had agreed to come on board as CEO. When Reed turned forty in four years, he'd take over as chairman as well. Another deal Reed had made with the controlling and manipulative Richard.

After what his parents had done to Marisa's life, Reed couldn't see himself ever working

in the family business. But he'd learned forgiveness from his sister and today he had a
decent relationship with his parents. It worked
as long as Richard stayed away and gave
Reed free rein. So it made him a little nervous when his father showed up for no reason.

"I have a golf date at the club in an hour,"
Richard said, as if reading Reed's mind. "I
wanted to stop by and tell you again how
pleased your mother and I are about your engagement. Daphne is a lovely young woman
and she will be a great asset to you."

Reed picked up the gold pen and studied it
again, something in his father's voice stinging
in a way he hadn't expected. "I'm not looking for an asset. We fell in love and we want
to be together to build a home and a family."

Richard nodded. "That's what I meant.
Your mother and I worried you'd be a bachelor forever."

Reed's father and mother had been es-
tranged for years. Vanessa Dalton had been
the only child of Harold Dalton, whose father had started the store in the early 1900s.
Richard had worked for Harold and had gone
after the beautiful Vanessa. Within months
they were married and Richard secured his
place in Dalton's and with Harold.

It wasn't a love match and soon after Marisa was born, Vanessa and Marisa moved to New York while Richard and Reed stayed in Dallas. That all changed when Marisa returned to Texas and found out about her daughter. Their mother soon followed and she and Richard were now sharing the home in Highland Park. Their marriage seemed strange to Reed, but he didn't question it. Who knew what their arrangement was?

"You can stop worrying."

Richard walked around the desk and patted Reed's shoulder. At six feet, Reed stood a little taller than his father, and Richard's hair was now a silver gray. Other than that, Reed knew they favored each other a great deal. Same color eyes and lean, sharp lines of the face and body. But Reed knew he hadn't inherited his father's cutthroat instincts or the do-anything attitude he used to get his way, uncaring of other people's feelings or lives.

"I'm proud of you, son. You've exceeded all my expectations."

Expectations! The word shot through him like a poison arrow. Something was always expected of him—to excel, to stay a step ahead of the competition, to make profits, to marry, to reproduce. He often wondered what it would feel like to be a man without everyone wanting something from him. What was it like to be free and unencumbered? Sometimes the yoke of responsibility weighed him down.

"Thank you," was all he could say. It wasn't easy living in his father's shadow, or as he liked to call it—living under his father's thumb.

"Your mother would like to have a dinner party for both families so Marisa and the kids can meet your soon-to-be in-laws."

It didn't escape Reed that his father hadn't mentioned Colter. "What about Colter?" No way was he letting him get away with that slight. Colter was wealthy in his own right, capitalizing on his winning name in the rodeo circuit. He now owned a boot company and supplied a lot of western stores. Dalton's carried his boots and other leather products and they were popular items.

Colter had character ingrained into his bones and he deserved Richard's respect. He'd devoted his life to Ellie when he'd thought Marisa hadn't wanted her. There wasn't a better father on this earth.

Richard frowned. "What?"

"You didn't mention Colter."

"Just an oversight," Richard said nonchalantly. "Colter is part of our family."

"Good. Just remember that."

"Son—"

"I'll talk to Mother when I get back." He cut off his father because he didn't want to rehash an old issue. He just wanted Richard to know he wouldn't tolerate leaving Colter out of anything. Neither would Marisa.

"Okay." Richard inclined his head. "Who's going with you on this trip?"

Reed knew his father was aware of everything he did. Richard had his sources—or spies—and Reed hadn't ferreted out the informant who told his father of his every move. He didn't spend a lot of time thinking about it because he had nothing to hide, but it irked him that Richard still had his finger on the pulse of this company. That implied Richard didn't trust him.

"Cari," he replied, watching his father's face, "I told Fletcher we'd take the small Learjet just in case you needed the bigger plane."

"Thanks, but we don't have any plans that I'm aware of. With your mother, though, that could change at a moment's notice." Richard rubbed his jaw in thought, his expression closed. "Ms. Michaels travels with you a great deal. Is that going to bother Daphne?"

There was that tone again. "No," Reed answered. "Just like it's not going to bother her when I travel with Monica."

"Monica's in her fifties."

Reed gritted his teeth, an old habit from his teen years when Richard tried to control his every move. "What are you getting at?"

"Ms. Michaels is a very attractive young woman."

"Yes, so?"

Richard shrugged and Reed didn't miss that look in his eyes. He'd seen it many times before.

"Ah." The light switch finally flipped on in his brain. "You're afraid I might have a romantic interest in Cari. That's why you're so happy. I chose the right woman—for a Preston."

The bar of acceptance was set high—only the very elite and wealthy were considered suitable partners for the Preston children. It was one of the reasons Reed had avoided marriage. He wouldn't subject a woman to that. But he'd gotten lucky with Daphne.

"Now, Reed, I didn't say that. You're very touchy today."

"Maybe I am," he conceded.

"Ms. Michaels holds a very important job in this company—a job she does very well. Her work ethic is exemplary and that's why I didn't object when you said you were promoting her to vice president when Frank retired. Besides, she's your sister's friend and she attends a lot of family functions."

"But she's not up to Richard Preston's standards for a wife for his son. Just like Colter wasn't an acceptable husband for Marisa." Reed tried to keep the anger out of his voice and failed.

"Son, you're getting angry for no reason."

"Yeah." Reed massaged the knot at the back of his neck. "But don't sugarcoat your feelings for my sake. You don't like Cari. It's very big of you to accept her for Marisa's benefit."

Richard stiffened. "I worked very hard to get where I am today. Is it a crime to want the best for my children?"

Reed's eyes didn't waver from Richard's and he could feel that old tension building inside him. "Yes, it's a crime when you use underhanded tactics and manipulation to achieve what you think is best for your children. Why don't you let them make their own decisions?"

"I do," Richard told him. "You and Marisa both know I'm the type of man who likes to be in control. But I've learned my lesson with Marisa. I'm not manipulating your lives anymore."

Reed jammed his hands into the pockets of his jeans. "We both appreciate that."

"But it doesn't stop me from being happy when you make good choices." His father's eyes gleamed and Reed realized not for the first time that Richard was a formidable opponent and an aggressive parent.

Before Reed could respond, Richard glanced at his watch. "I've got to run." He walked to the door in his quick easy strides. "Do you and Daphne have plans for the weekend?"

"We're visiting her parents at their lake house in Austin."

"Don't forget to call your mother about the party."

"I won't," Reed responded to an empty doorway.

He walked over and closed the door, resisting the urge to slam it. Something about making his father so happy left a bad taste in his mouth.

But he'd get over it.

Cari made the limo on time. She handed the driver her bag and slid onto the plush leather seat across from Reed.

"Glad you found shoes," he remarked, staring at her heels with a lift of his brow.

"It helps working for a department store and having everything at my disposal." She crossed her legs and scooted farther over. Reed's legs were so long that she didn't want to bump his knees. His dark gaze made the space between them seem that much smaller.

"Mmm." He rubbed his chin and against her will she watched his strong lean fingers stroke his rough male skin. A hint of his cologne, sort of a musk mingled with leather, wafted to her, and a wave of pleasure rippled in her stomach.

"Any ill effects from the fall?"

For a moment she didn't even catch the question, but she recovered quickly. She placed her Chanel bag, a gift from Dalton's, beside her on the seat for something to do. "No. By midmorning my aches and pains were gone. But my pride is still bruised, and you can bet someone is going to answer for that defective heel."

"And if you have your way, that brand of shoe won't be carried in Dalton's anymore?"

"You got it. I have George looking into it and I'll have all the details on your desk Monday morning."

Reed kept staring at her, and she wondered if her lipstick was smeared. She resisted the urge to grab her compact.

"What?"

He leaned forward. "Do you know your eyes glow when you're passionate about something?"

"Is there smoke coming out of my ears, too?" She had to be flippant or she was going to lose what little control she had.

Reed laughed—a deep throaty sound that felt as exhilarating as sliding her dad's old truck's stick shift into third gear. As a teenager she knew she was off for the ride of her life. As an adult, Reed's laugh gave her a glimpse of a ride she was never going to experience.

She stared out the window as the car whipped through traffic. Soon the driver turned into the entrance for Love Field where the Dalton jets were housed. Everything was arranged so there was no waiting. Within minutes they boarded the plane. Fletcher and Melody, the pilots, welcomed them aboard.

Cari had made many company trips. Two pilots were required to fly the plane, even the smaller Learjet. Melody was the only female copilot who worked for Dalton's, and Cari admired her venture into mostly a man's profession. The interior of the plane was lavish, with ebony wood and Italian leather, made to cater to the very rich. It had been decorated and customized per Richard Preston's request. Cari always felt a little out of place when she stepped onto the lush wool carpet of the living-room style cabin.

She eased onto a small sofa, placed her purse and briefcase beside her and buckled up for takeoff. Reed spoke to Fletcher and took a tan captain's chair across from her. The plane could easily seat six people.

"We're ready to go," Reed said, adjusting his seat belt.

Soon they were taxiing down the runway and the jet lifted from the tarmac with a smoothness that still left butterflies in her stomach. Her fear of heights always made her stomach knot with tension, but she generally managed to control it. Up, up they went into the fluffy white clouds, leaving Dallas behind.

Once the plane was in the air, Melody left her seat. "Everything is going smoothly. May I get you something to drink?" Another thing Cari liked about Melody, she was always willing to please. Her job was being a pilot but she didn't consider it beneath her to act as a flight attendant. Cari had a feeling the woman was going to go far in life.

Tearing her eyes away from the window and that vast nothingness of space, Cari unbuckled her seat belt. "Water, please."

"Me, too," Reed replied, resting one booted foot over his knee.

Melody served the drinks on a silver tray with Waterford crystal. Cari often thought this was the height of ostentation, but it was the norm for the Prestons.

As Reed took his glass, he said, "Melody, you really don't have to do this."

"It's my pleasure." Melody smiled so brightly it was blinding.

He's engaged, Cari wanted to say. Women were always flirting with him. That was the norm, too.

"Thank you," Reed said, and Melody floated back to the cockpit.

They rode in silence for a moment.

She could feel Reed's eyes on her and she refused to squirm. Finally he asked, "What do you think of Daphne?"

She swallowed, choosing her words carefully. "She's very beautiful."

He idly rubbed his leather boot, his eyes watching her. "I sense a 'but'…"

Her eyes caught his. "I hadn't realized you were dating anyone seriously." The words were like puffs of air she couldn't capture or take back.

His eyes darkened. "I'm not aware I have to clear my dating schedule with you."

His spurt of anger didn't deter her. "I work closely with you every day and I'm wondering why you felt a need to keep Daphne a secret."

"My personal life is my business."

"So what do you care what I think of Daphne?"

"Sir." Fletcher's voice came through on the intercom. "We're going through a thunderstorm, so there'll be some turbulence. Nothing serious."

Water splattered against the window and Cari turned her attention to it. The small plane trembled and faltered from the impact of the rain and the wind. Lightning split the sky, illuminating the cabin. It was too close.

She turned her thoughts to Reed. No way would she tell him how she felt about him. He loved Daphne and blurting out her feelings would only complicate things between them.

"Cari…"

She heard his throaty voice and she couldn't look at him. She wasn't that strong.

Instead, she placed her water on a side table and then opened her briefcase. She focused her attention on the itinerary and the conversation turned to business, something they both were more comfortable with.

"I see you've planned to take the manager and his staff out to dinner," she said.

"Yes, the store is doing very well. I wanted to do something special, but I'm afraid I'll have to cut it short. I plan to return to Dallas tonight."

She knew why.

She didn't need the overnight bag, but she still liked to carry one to freshen up. "They'll appreciate the thought," she replied.

A tense pause followed her words.

"Cari…"

Why couldn't he let it go? She didn't want to talk about his engagement or Daphne.

"Sir," Fletcher's voice came through, more urgent this time, "we're losing power, so it might be best if everyone buckled up."

"What the hell?" Reed sprang from his seat and made his way to the cockpit. Cari could hear them clearly. "What's the problem?" Reed asked.

"I'm trying to get the plane above the thunderstorm, but we're losing power," Fletcher replied.

"Both engines?"

"Just one, sir."

"Were we hit by lightning?"

"That's my guess. I'm trying to restart the engine."

Cari looked out the window and she could tell they were going down. Fear leaped into her throat and she quickly fastened her seat belt.

Melody was trying to help Fletcher, but the plane was not responding.

"Damn it, man," Reed yelled. "Do something."

"Mayday, Mayday. We have a problem." Fletcher spouted off altitude and longitude and other flight facts, but it didn't keep the plane from careening off course and downward.

The sound of thunder cracked loudly and the remaining engine died away. "We've lost contact and power," Fletcher shouted. "I'm beginning a descent for ditching. Without power the plane cannot stay in the air. We have to land in a remote location. Take your seat, sir. Now!"

The plane wobbled severely and continued to glide slowly toward the ground. Cari began to pray and a scream clogged her throat.

Reed jumped into his seat, his face pale. He stared into her eyes and she saw more in that instant than she had in all the years she'd known him. She saw the fear and she also saw something else. As the plane jerked and spun they knew it was too late.

For them.

They were going to die.

Chapter Three

Cari awoke to pain and a throbbing in her head. Not another Tylenol morning. She opened her eyes and the pain was overtaken by fear.

Where was she?

Something held her in place. A seat belt. Was she in her car? No. She was jammed against something hard and a heavy object was on top of her. Opening her eyes more she saw wires hanging from the ceiling, compartments flung open, items strewn everywhere. She was covered in debris.

The plane had crashed!

Everything came flooding back.

Melody lay in the doorway to the cockpit and she could see Fletcher slumped over in his seat. The nose of the plane had been pushed forward and the instrument panel pressed against the pilot. She didn't know if he was dead or alive.

An eerie quiet filled the cabin.

Reed!

Raising her head, she winced and noticed blood on her hand. A shard of glass stuck out of the soft flesh near her thumb. She bit her lip, pulled it out and held her hand against her chest to stop the bleeding. Otherwise she was okay. Or at least she thought she was, just cuts, bruises and aches.

Reed's chair was twisted and his head rested against the side of the cabin, which seemed to be tilted and crushed in slightly. He was bleeding, his shirt soaked with bright red.

Ohmygod!

He needed help. She pushed debris off her and managed to unsnap her seat belt. As she struggled to her feet a wave of dizziness assailed her. The plane wasn't level, so it made the dizziness worse. The cabin was pushed together and there was very little room. She gripped the wobbly captain's chair and reached for the pulse in Reed's neck. She didn't find one. Ohmygod! No!

Take a deep breath. Stay focused.

Trying to keep her nerves from spiraling out of control, she stepped over more debris and made her way to Melody by holding on to parts of the shattered plane. The cabin was so mangled Cari couldn't stand upright. She knelt by Melody, checking her pulse. None. Blood oozed from her head. Cari wouldn't let herself think as she frantically tried to reach Fletcher. Parts of the plane dangled from above, blocking her reach. Then she smelled it.

Fuel.

Smoke.

Ohmygod!

Stay focused! They need you.

The door of the plane had been ripped away. She peered outside. A chilly foreboding swept over her and she trembled. The crushed plane was balancing precariously on a ledge or a mountain. She knew they had to get out and get out fast.

Her high heels crunched on Waterford crystal. She had a sudden urge to laugh hysterically—but she had to get them out. She couldn't fall apart.

It was hard to stay balanced in her heels, but there was glass everywhere, so she couldn't remove them. She unsnapped Reed's seat belt and shook him. "Reed, wake up. Please, wake up." He didn't move or make a sound. Blood dripped from his head onto her hands. She grabbed a towel from the floor and wrapped it tightly around his head and then she pulled and dragged him as close to the door as she could. He weighed a ton but she never paused in her struggle. Once there, she placed his arms halfway out the door.

She glanced down, kicked off her heels and jumped. Since the door was tilted down, she misjudged the distance and almost fell flat on her face. Pain shot through her body, but she quickly scrambled to her feet. Looking up, she caught her breath. The opening seemed so far away. The plane was a mangled mess. How was she still living? Oh God! She had to take several deep breaths.

Focus! Focus!

She had to get Reed and the others out before the plane ignited. She stood on her tiptoes until she could grab Reed's hands, and then she tugged and tugged with all her strength. Slowly, she inched him forward. Catching her breath, she reached for his armpits and dragged him out. Once his weight shifted, his body slid forward quickly and took them both to the ground. She struggled to her feet and grabbed hold of him once again. Her muscles strained and her arms burned, but she jerked and pulled until she had him safely away from the shattered plane.

Now she had to get Melody and Fletcher. Taking a deep breath, she sprinted back toward the plane. A loud explosion flung her backward. Flames roared through the crumpled fuselage.

No! No!

The excessive heat yanked her from the abyss of terror. She rose and pulled Reed farther away from the flames. Then she collapsed into a ball of fear, her body trembling uncontrollably.

She drew her knees to her chin. Wrapping her arms around her legs, she tried to stop the tremors. In a chilled stupor, she watched the smoldering plane until nothing was left but a melted heap of twisted metal.

Hot, smoldering metal.

The rain had stopped, so there was nothing to cool the offensive heat. She didn't know how long she sat there lost somewhere between Dallas and this horrendous nightmare.

When reality returned, tears were streaming down her cheeks and she was holding Reed's hand.

Praying.

Praying for a pulse. Praying he was alive. But he just seemed cold. The towel was soaked with blood, but it looked as if the bleeding might have stopped. That was good. More tears followed. She cried for Fletcher and Melody and she cried for life's cruel injustice. After a moment she pulled herself together.

Looking around, it seemed as if they were on a crater of the moon—dirt and rocks and nothing else except an endless sky. Not the moon, but probably a mountain somewhere in west Texas.

They had to just wait and someone would find them.

Someone would rescue them.

She prayed it was in time to save Reed.

Richard Preston hung up the phone as his wife, Vanessa, entered his study.

"Are you ready?" she asked. Even in her late fifties she was still an attractive woman with blond hair and a svelte figure flattered by a Vera Wang suit. She had the body of a dancer and she never grew tired of reminding him of what she'd given up for marriage and motherhood. He wasn't going to think about that, though. They were getting along and their children were happy. Life was good.

"I don't feel like going to the Maxwells' for dinner," he said, testing the waters. The Maxwells were her ballet friends and they bored him to death with endless chatter about the next greatest dancer to grace Lincoln Center.

When she frowned, he quickly added, "I just got off the phone with Clyde Harwood. He and Muriel are planning an engagement party for Reed and Daphne. They would like a list of guests by the end of the week."

"So." She lifted a finely arched eyebrow. "An evening with friends isn't going to delay the list. Admit it, you just don't want to go."

"Maybe. I'm all keyed up about Reed's engagement and I would prefer to stay home. Our son has made an excellent choice. Daphne is a charming, sophisticated young lady who will do the Preston name proud."

"Yes, Daphne will make Reed an exceptional wife."

Richard stood. "I was worried he'd fall for Cari Michaels."

"Cari's a nice girl and a very good friend to Marisa."

"But she's not suitable as a wife for our son."

Vanessa sighed. "Oh, Richard, haven't you learned your lesson? We almost lost Marisa and I will not tolerate you doing anything to jeopardize Reed's happiness."

"That's what is so wonderful. Reed made the perfect choice all on his own."

"I don't know. Marisa seems to have reservations and I trust her instincts. I just hope Reed is as deeply in love as our daughter."

"He is. You can see it."

Vanessa nodded. "They make a lovely couple. Marisa is very fond of Cari and I think she's more disappointed Reed and Cari didn't get together than anything else."

Richard smiled at his wife. "That's it. Reed made a choice without pressure from Marisa or me. That's why I'm so excited and would rather stay home to go over the guest list. It will be the party of the year."

She lifted an eyebrow again. "Maybe. Get your jacket. You're going tonight. We have something to celebrate."

"Vanessa…"

A tap at the door stopped him. Winston, the

butler, stepped in. "Sir, there's a gentleman here to see you, a Mr. Darin Avery, a representative from the regional office of the National Transportation Safety Board."

Richard frowned. "What does he want? Is there a problem with the plane?"

"I don't know, sir. Would you like for me to send him in?"

"Yes."

A balding man with a worried expression walked in. "Mr. and Mrs. Richard Preston?"

"Yes," Richard replied. "What's this about?"

"I regret to inform you the Dalton jet went down at 1439 hours somewhere in west Texas."

Richard felt a blow to his chest. "What?"

"No!" Vanessa screamed and Winston rushed in.

"As soon as the weather clears, we'll have planes in the air searching for the wreckage. I just wanted to let you know before the story broke on the news. You have my deepest regrets."

"My son...my son, is he alive?" Vanessa asked, holding on to Winston.

"We don't know, ma'am, but—"

"Don't say it," Richard shouted. "My son is alive. He has to be."

"I'll be in touch, sir." He laid a card on the desk. "If you need anything, you can reach me on my cell." He walked out.

"Richard…"

"Vanessa, just stay calm."

"Calm!" she screeched. "Our son has just gone down in a plane. I can be as emotional as I want! I have to call Marisa. I need Marisa."

She reached for the phone as Winston handed her a glass of brandy.

Richard sank into his chair, refusing to believe his son was anything but alive. He had to be. His whole future was waiting for him.

A future Richard had precisely planned.

Cari removed the towel from Reed's head. A cut zigzagged across his left temple and a dark bruise spread from his ear to his hairline, but the bleeding had stopped. Since she didn't have anything else, she wrapped the blood-caked towel around his head again.

Soon someone would come.

Reed's sun-browned skin was so pale, and she checked his pulse. A faint beat trembled against her fingers.

"Reed!" she shouted in joy. "Can you hear me? Reed!"

A low moan escaped his throat and she cupped his face. "Reed."

The moan grew stronger and his eyelids fluttered. Excitement ran through her. He was alive! She continued to call his name until his eyes slowly opened.

"Ca-ri."

"Yes, yes!" Without thinking, she kissed his cheek. She was just so glad he was alive.

"Wh-ere are we?"

"The plane crashed and I'm guessing we're somewhere in west Texas."

"Wh-ere's Fletcher and Melody?"

When she didn't answer, he sat up and groaned, grabbing his head.

"Take it easy."

He caught sight of the pile of twisted, burned metal. "Is...is...that...?"

She swallowed. "Yes. That's all that's left of the plane."

"Oh my God! How did we get out?"

"I pulled you out."

"Fletcher and Melody?" His voice was hopeful despite the anguish imprinted on his face.

"I was going back to get them when the

plane exploded, but they…were…already dead." She had to believe that.

He buried his face in his blood-covered hands. She wrapped her arms around him. "A rescue team should be here soon."

He raised his head. "But not in time for Fletcher and Melody."

"No." She felt his tears as they dripped onto her cheek and she tightened her arms, her face buried in his chest. His arms went around her like a vise and they grieved for the two people they'd lost. They sat that way minutes or maybe hours. She wasn't sure, but the light was fading. Raindrops peppered their heads. They had to find shelter.

She untangled from him and stood, surveying the desolate, bare scenery. They were in the middle of nowhere and as she looked out, she saw more of the same. More mountains, more desolate landscape.

"What are you doing?"

"We have to find shelter for the time being." She glanced toward the darkening sky. "It looks like another thunderstorm is on the way. Stay here. I'm going to scout around."

"Cari…"

"I'll be okay, Reed. Just rest. You've lost a lot of blood."

"I can't seem to do much else at the moment," he replied in a low voice.

She walked away on the uneven terrain in her stocking feet. Several deep indentations had been hollowed out in the mountain from the elements. They could possibly use one as a cave until a search party arrived.

Lastly, she moved toward the charred wreckage. Pieces still smoldered. She didn't know what she was hoping to find. Something. Anything. She peered over the side of the mountain. A wing from the plane, a wheel, objects she couldn't identify and several personal items had been thrown free.

A backpack caught her eye. If there was clothing inside she could use it to bandage Reed's wound. The backpack was on a steep incline going down to nowhere. Could she reach it?

Ever since she fell out of a tree as a kid, she'd had a fear of heights. Flying had been a challenge, but her job was important to her so she had conquered it. Now she had to find the courage to crawl down and retrieve the pack.

Reed was still sitting with his head buried on his knees, so weak and needing medical attention. Without a second thought, she turned around and inched down the side of the mountain. Her stocking feet were a problem. Damn, she should have removed them, but she wasn't climbing back up to do that. Luckily she was able to find footholds on clumps of dirt and rocks, which scratched the bottom of her feet. But she kept going.

As she put pressure on one rock, it came loose and tumbled down, carrying a load of dirt with it. Cari closed her eyes, sucked in a breath and held on to a scraggly bush for dear life. Dust clogged her sinuses and she tasted it in her mouth along with her fear. She took a long ragged breath, said a prayer and found another foothold.

Finally she reached the backpack. It was pink and black, so she knew it must have belonged to Melody. With one hand she reached for it and slipped one arm through. Then she did the same with the other arm. Tentatively, she started the trek back up.

She climbed over the top as raindrops started to fall. Staggering to her feet, she ran to Reed.

"We have to find shelter," she said, plopping down beside him.

He raised his head and his eyes were unfocused, dazed, and she wondered if he was going to pass out. "Wh-at?"

Slipping an arm around his waist, she asked, "Can you stand?" Within minutes she had him on his feet, but he swayed. With a fierce grip she led him to the partial cave that had a slight overhang. Just as she did, the heavens opened and torrential rain splattered the terrain.

She shrugged off the backpack and placed it on the ground. Reed slumped against her and she watched as the rain beat down on the wreckage.

After a moment she turned her attention to Reed. He probably had a concussion, so she had to keep him awake. She shook him several times and kept talking, but he was so out of it she finally gave up. Her strength was waning, too. The sound of the rain was hypnotic and she drifted into an exhausted, restless sleep.

Marisa Kincaid hurried into her father's study followed by her husband. "Have you heard anything?"

"No, sweetheart, we're still waiting," Richard replied.

"Where's Mother?"

"She's in her room. The doctor sedated her, but I'm sure she'd be happy to see you. Actually, she keeps calling for you."

"I'll go right up." She turned and then pivoted to face Richard. "Have you notified Cari's family?"

"No. I thought I'd wait until we heard something definite."

"I suppose that's best." His daughter's face crumpled and Richard saw the first crack in her strong facade. Colter put his arm around her and she clung to him.

Richard didn't think he was ever going to get used to this cowboy being his son-in-law. Marisa had her choice of the most eligible bachelors in the country, yet she chose a rodeo cowboy. For his daughter and grandchildren, he tried his best to like the man. And he wasn't so bad. Colter had a lot of qualities Richard admired: responsibility, honesty and loyalty. It was his blue-collar roots that got Richard.

Daphne stepped into the room. "Has there been any news?"

Now, *there* was class and breeding, a woman who had it all. How he wished Marisa had made such a good choice.

"I'm afraid not," Richard answered. "The weather is still a factor."

Marisa wiped away a tear and looked at Daphne. "You're taking this very well."

"Of course. It's not going to do me any good to fall apart."

"Yes. Heaven forbid," Marisa said and walked out.

Colter twisted his hat. "Her brother and her best friend are probably dead, so you can understand her state of mind." He placed his hat on his head. "Or maybe not." Saying that, he followed Marisa.

"What did he mean?" Daphne asked.

"Never mind. Everyone is a little emotional." Richard walked to her. "How are you, my dear?"

"I'm okay." She glanced at her watch. "I have an interview at a TV station in about an hour, so I better go."

"Do you think that's wise?"

"It's better than them hounding me. I'll give them an interview and they'll leave me alone."

"Maybe so."

She hugged him and quickly left. Something bothered Richard and he couldn't explain what it was. In the face of trauma,

Daphne was a real trooper. Once Reed returned, he would be happy to hear that.

Wouldn't he?

Cari woke up to an ache in every bone in her body. Darkness surrounded them, but a brilliant moon hung in the sky like a huge night-light. If she held out her hand, she was sure she could touch its golden rim.

Everything felt like a nightmare and she didn't have to wonder if she was awake because she knew she was. Every ache and bruise told her that in triplicate.

She winced as pain shot up her back. She did a double take when she found Reed staring at her. His breath fanned her cheek and the fear inside her eased.

"Oh." She smiled. "You're better."

"Thanks to you I'm alive."

A palpable silence ensued and she rushed into speech. "How's your head?"

He grimaced. "Pounding. But I don't feel as weak. I've been watching you sleep for some time."

She frowned. "Did I snore?"

"No, not that I noticed." He glanced to the vastness of the night. "It's beautiful, isn't it?"

"If I was looking at it on TV in my living room, yes, it would be spectacular. But seeing it after surviving a plane crash is just nightmarish."

"I know what you mean." He shifted to stretch out his long legs. "At least the rain has stopped. Surely someone will be here in the morning to rescue us."

"Yeah." Cari thought of her parents. "I wonder if our families have been notified of the crash."

"Probably. I hope someone is with Daphne. She'll take this hard. And Marisa. God, she doesn't need any more heartache."

"She has Colter. He'll be right there with her."

"Mmm. You're right. Colter is solid as a rock. He'll take care of my sister."

She was silent for a moment with thoughts of her own.

"What?" Reed asked.

"I was just thinking about my parents." She moved to get more comfortable against the dirt wall. "My folks say I have highfalutin ideas and have strayed from my roots. They get upset when I miss family functions for business. Sunday is my dad's birthday and this time I planned not to miss it. But…" She drew a deep breath. "I guess I will."

"Hey." One finger touched her cheek and it warmed her whole body. "We'll be out of here by Sunday."

"Maybe."

"Tell me about your parents. You don't speak about your family much."

Didn't she? She thought she did.

"My relationship with my father is strained. He was absent so much of my childhood and as a kid, I didn't understand that. He was in the fields or the barn before we woke up. Work didn't stop until there was no more daylight, and then because Hill County was dry he'd drive to the next county and drink with his farming buddies."

Reed didn't say anything so she continued. "When he returned home, we were all asleep, except my mom. She'd wait up, keeping his supper warm. Then a loud argument would erupt, waking all of us. My mom was a quiet, hardworking woman, but she wasn't afraid to voice her opinions."

"Well, I know where you get that from then."

"Mmm." She lifted an eyebrow, but didn't comment on the comparison. "My mother is a strong lady. She would tell my father he needed to be home with his family instead of drinking with his friends. His kids needed to see him. If my dad had had one drink too many then there was a lot of yelling and cursing. Usually Dad stormed out and slept in the barn." She brushed dust from her slacks.

"Kitty, Judith and I shared a room and on those nights we'd cuddle close, all of us afraid our parents were going to divorce. But the next morning things were back to normal and Dad was at the kitchen table for breakfast with us."

"Sounds like a typical American family."

"There were so many arguments, though, and I never understood a man who was not there for his children. As I grew older I realized the enormous responsibility my father carried, especially when the crops failed and his family had to depend on the goodwill of others to get by. Sam Michaels never shared any of his pain. He kept it all inside."

She took a deep breath. "My mother was a marvel, loving her husband and putting up with his attitudes and behavior. As mad as she sometimes got at him, she always had his meals on the table. Now, *that* I really didn't understand. As a teenager I vowed I would never have a relationship like that."

"No matter his faults, she loved him," Reed

said. "That's why she had his meals ready. She knew how hard he worked and she knew his sorrow. But it didn't keep her from getting angry."

"Yeah." From his viewpoint he could see it so clearly. Her parents were partners through the good and the bad. As a child she had wanted it all to be good. No family ever was. She loved her family and it was always fun to see them. Being with her father on his birthday took on more meaning than it ever had.

"I know you have brothers and sisters."

She drew her knees up. "Sammy, the oldest, works the farm with our father. He and his wife, Janice, and their two sons live in our grandparents' old house. Judith, my oldest sister, married a neighboring farmer's son and they live close by with their two girls. Kitty, my other sister, followed me to Dallas, and as hard as I tried I couldn't get her to go to college. She said it wasn't for her, so she went to beauty school, met Charlie and got married. They live in a Dallas suburb. Chase is the baby and still a bachelor. After getting his degree, he went to work for a large oil company and travels all over the world."

She could hardly believe she was telling Reed all this. "My father has never come out and said it, but I know he blames me for luring Kitty and Chase away from their roots."

"That's probably just your imagination."

"Maybe."

Despite the tension between her and her father there was always something cathartic about going home.

Would she ever be home again?

As they talked, the sun rose like a blaze of fire over the mountains. They sat in wonder as dawn crept over the turbulent landscape, revealing its harshness and untamed uniqueness.

With a groan she scrambled out of the cave. Something scurried across her foot and she screamed.

"What is it?" Reed followed her out, his face a mask of pain.

"Some critter or something." She closed her eyes. "I don't want to know what it was. I just want out of this godforsaken place. Why isn't there someone here to rescue us? It's been hours."

He slipped his arms around her. "Don't fall apart on me."

"I'm afraid, Reed." She rested her head on his chest. "I'm so afraid and I don't have any shoes."

He glanced at her feet. "What happened to your shoes?"

"I kicked off my heels when I jumped out of the plane. I figured I'd break my neck if I didn't and I had enough problems."

"Cari. Cari." He stroked her hair. "We've been through a horrendous ordeal and it's normal to be afraid. But we're alive. Soon we'll be back with our loved ones and you'll have a storeful of shoes at your disposal. We just have to be patient."

Loved ones. Daphne.

She didn't feel the pain of that. It had taken a plane crash to get her thoughts straight. She and Reed Preston were worlds apart and she wasn't living in a dream world anymore. This dose of reality was more than she needed. The trip had started out with a broken heart. Now she just wanted to survive, go home and find happiness in her own world.

They both stared at the charred spot where the plane had crashed. The rain and wind had pushed the fuselage down the side of the mountain like garbage.

"This is going to make the plane harder to find," Reed said, trying not to lose his confidence. "It's amazing how a big thing like that can just disappear."

"They must have ways to locate crashed aircraft."

"I sincerely hope so." Reed rubbed his hands together. "If we just had water and a good breakfast, the wait might be more bearable. I'm so thirsty."

"Oh. Oh." Cari ran back to the cave and came out with the backpack. "I found this on the side of the mountain after the crash."

"Did you climb down to get it?"

"Yes, and since I'm afraid of heights, it was no small feat."

"I never knew that." She hid her feelings well. She'd always given the impression of being fearless.

"Oh, there's a lot you don't know about me."

He felt he knew all the things that were important, like her dedication, her loyalty and her bravery.

She knelt and unzipped the backpack. "Oh, my, shoes." Excited as a child, she held up the white-and-pink sneakers. "Just what I wanted and it's not even Christmas."

He watched the gleam in her eyes as she

shoved a foot into a shoe. Her face fell. "It's too big. Damn. What size are these?"

Cari suddenly became still and silent.

"What is it?"

"They're Melody's and…"

"Cari, you did everything you could."

"I know. It's just sad."

Simultaneously they took a moment to remember Melody and Fletcher.

Cari then found socks in the bag and slipped them on. "Much better," she said, walking around in the shoes. Her slacks, suit jacket, blouse and hair were stained with blood and dirt. Reed thought she'd never looked lovelier.

He picked up the pack. Two bottles of water and high-protein cereal bars were a welcome sight. "Breakfast," he said, easing to the ground.

They decided to save one bottle for later. He handed her a bar and she broke it in half and handed him a piece. They sat in comfortable silence eating what they had. The water tasted heavenly.

She licked her lips. "Well, Junior, now what do we do?"

He smiled. She hadn't called him that in a long time. "We wait."

By the end of the day they were still waiting, staring at the expanse of sky, fighting not to drink the rest of the water. There was nothing but a clear blue that went on forever. No planes. No helicopters. No rescue team. It was almost as if they'd been forgotten.

And he and Cari were the only two people in the universe.

Cari used a cotton T-shirt from the bag to change his bandage. She said the wound was already healing. All he knew was the pounding in his head wasn't so severe.

He noticed her red hands. "Did you burn your hands?"

She flexed her fingers. "I guess it happened when the plane exploded. They just burn a little."

She'd hurt herself trying to save the others and she hadn't said a word. In that moment he realized what an incredible person she was and he wanted to do something to help her. He did the only thing he could. He took her hands and kissed the reddened parts.

A fleeting smile touched her lips. "Ah, much better." The smile quickly faded. "They're not going to find us, are they?" Her voice seemed to come from a long way off.

"Doesn't look like it. The plane must have

been way off course. No telling where they're searching."

"What do we do?"

Reed glanced at his watch for the first time. The crystal was broken and it had stopped. At 2:39 p.m. The time of the crash. He removed it and laid it on the ground. It wasn't much good to him now. He stood and surveyed the landscape. "We walk off this mountain. Are you ready?"

She rose to her feet. "I have shoes. I'm ready."

Reed narrowed his eyes against the late-evening sun. "You wouldn't by any chance have been a Girl Scout?"

"No. Why?"

"I'm trying to figure out which way to go. El Paso would be west, Mexico south, so we want to go east. Right?"

"That sounds logical. West would be nothing but more desolate landscape. South and north would be out of the question, too far to find civilization. East is our only hope of finding a small town or ranch."

"The sun is sinking in the west so we want to go that direction." He pointed east. "We have to wait until morning though. Starting at night is not a good idea and maybe by morning we'll get lucky and they'll find us."

"Back to the cave?"

"Just in case it rains again."

"I hope it does," she said. "I'd stand out here with my mouth open."

"I'd join you," he told her. "For now let's try not to think about water."

They walked toward the hollowed spot in the mountain. All of a sudden they heard a swooshing sound overhead.

Cari looked up. "Ohmygod, bats!" She sank to the ground and covered her head.

"What are you doing?"

"I don't want them in my hair."

"Cari, that's just a myth. Thcy're leaving their roost to feed at night. Unless you have insects in your hair, you're safe."

She rose to her feet. "That's not funny."

He gently touched her cheek. "I'm sorry. I can't believe you're afraid of bats."

She shuddered. "At the moment I'm afraid of everything."

He put his arm around her and they settled into the hollowed cave. "I'll protect you from the bats," he said. "I can handle that."

But there were so many unknowns out here and he wondered if they'd be able to survive.

He had to be strong for her. The air was a bit chilly. Last night they'd been exhausted and hadn't noticed. He slipped off his jacket and they used it as a blanket.

She snuggled against him. "I always wondered if I had all the time in the world, what I would do."

"And…"

"Mmm. Soak in a hot Jacuzzi in my luxury private bathroom, sipping wine, eating chocolate-covered strawberries and watching a movie on my big-screen TV, which is a fantasy because I don't have any of those things."

"What male movie star would be in this Jacuzzi with you?"

She grew thoughtful. "Ah. George Clooney for sure. Johnny Depp would work. Hugh Jackman also. Ethan Hawke, too."

"I get the picture."

As darkness fell there was silence for a moment and their situation intruded.

"Reed…"

"Go to sleep, Cari. Tomorrow's another day."

"Tomorrow's my dad's birthday."

"One way or the other we'll get out of here

and you can wish your dad happy birthday in person."

He intended to keep that promise for the woman who'd saved his life.

Chapter Four

Richard paced in his study while Mr. Avery unrolled a map on his desk. Marisa and Colter stood nearby, anxiously awaiting whatever information the man could give them. Vanessa sat on the sofa, her eyes glazed from medication.

"The Dalton Learjet is equipped with an Emergency Locator Transmitter which should have sent out a signal for rescue upon impact, but it didn't. The ELT operates off a 9-volt battery pack and we've come to the conclusion that either the battery was dead or low."

"Damn it." Richard ran a hand through his hair, angry and frustrated.

Mr. Avery pointed to the map. "The plane veered severely off the flight plan and that's our problem. The last contact we had was here." He jabbed his finger at an area around Pecos. "West Texas is vast and we have helicopters in the air searching. So far nothing. It's like finding a needle in a haystack."

"But there's still hope?" Marisa asked.

"Mrs. Kincaid, the elements out there are harsh and—"

"Yes, there's hope," Richard intervened. The man didn't need to upset his daughter.

"Mr. Preston, it's been forty-eight hours. The Michaels family has been notified and the pilots' families as well."

Marisa turned to Winston, standing at the door. "Send a car to the Michaels family to bring them here to wait for news."

"Marisa, there's no need for that," Richard quickly said. "I'm sure the Michaelses would rather be in their own home."

Marisa's eyes darkened. "Do you have something against them coming here?"

"No. I just think they'll feel out of place."

"I see. Then I'll just go to them."

"No." Vanessa jumped to her feet. "Winston, send a car. I do not want Marisa to leave this house. The Michaelses are welcome here."

"Thank you, Mother. I'll call Ruth and Sam and speak to them myself."

"Honey." Colter reached for Marisa's arm as she made to leave the room.

She leaned into him. "I'm fine, really."

He pulled her into his arms and held her. Richard had to respect the way Colter loved and cared for his girl.

Colter cupped her face. "I'll go and get them. Since I've met them they'll probably feel more comfortable with me than with a stranger."

"Thank you." Marisa threw her arms around his neck.

"Give them a call so they'll know I'm coming."

As he walked out, Marisa reached for her cell and went into another room.

Vanessa looked around. "Where's Daphne? I thought she was here."

"She had to go out, but she'll be back."

"That's strange." Vanessa held on to the sofa for support. "I'll speak to Thelma so she can prepare rooms." She glanced at him, her eyes clearer than they had been all day. "If you do anything to upset Marisa or the Michaelses, you'll answer to me."

"I'm not thoughtless." How he wished he could be more like Colter and able to comfort his wife, but that wasn't in his nature. For the first time he saw that flaw.

"Maybe just insensitive," Vanessa remarked.

Before he could respond, Marisa came back and Vanessa reached for her, hugging her tightly. "Darling, how many rooms do you think we'll need?"

Marisa brushed back her hair. "I had a hard time convincing them, but they finally agreed. Let's see, Ruth and Sam, their son Sammy and their daughter Judith. Their other son Chase is in Midland and he's on the way. Kitty lives in Dallas and should be here any minute."

"I'll have Thelma prepare the west wing so they'll have plenty of room."

"Thank you, Mother." Marisa brushed back her hair again, a sign she was upset. "I feel better with them here. Closer to Cari."

Vanessa touched her face. "I know, darling. Now, let's go make arrangements."

They left Richard standing there and at that

moment he felt truly alone. That shocked him. He wasn't a sentimental person.

For Cari and Reed the morning came with startling reality. No search team was coming. The sky was empty and the only sound was of the dry west Texas wind.

They ate the last cereal bar and drank the last of the water, savoring each drop. Cari stuffed the bottle into the pack, then slipped her arms through the holes and adjusted it to ride easily on her back. Reed wrapped his jacket around his waist. They began the trek down the mountain to find civilization.

Reed took the lead and stumbled and slid several times because the terrain was so treacherous. Rocks and holes impeded their progress.

Cari stopped and knelt to tie her sneakers tighter. Her heels burned and she was afraid the big shoes were giving her blisters. Reed seemed to have no problem in his cowboy boots. They trudged on, but Cari was growing tired. So was Reed. They paused to take a breather, sitting on some sort of patchy dried dirt.

They had no water. They had nothing and

Cari wondered how long they could survive without food or something to drink.

"How are you doing?" Reed asked, looking like a sheikh with the T-shirt wrapped around his head.

"I'm fine under the circumstances." She rose to her knees and undid the T-shirt to check his wound. The shirt was filthy and his hair was caked with blood, but the jagged cut was healing nicely if infection didn't set in.

"You're a fast healer."

He was silent for a moment. "Why did you pull me from the plane first?"

She sat back on her heels, the question taking her by surprise. There was a saying about saving the one you love. Or was it loving the one you're with? Either way she couldn't explain it.

She shrugged. "I didn't know if you were dead or alive and I figured Melody was dead. I couldn't get to Fletcher so I got you out as fast as I could."

His eyes held hers. "Thank you."

She swallowed. "You're welcome." She stuffed the dirty shirt inside the backpack to hide her nervousness and pulled out a red scarf. "This should work to protect your cut."

She tied the bright scarf around his head

and surveyed him. "Definitely a Johnny Depp look."

He grinned. "All we need is a Jacuzzi."

"From your mouth to God's ear." She tried to be flip but the light in his eyes was doing strange things to her stomach. Or it could be hunger pains. Or thirst. She stood. "We better keep going."

They slowly made their way down and Cari faltered a time or two, but she kept up. Reed had a hard time, too, and she knew his head must be hurting.

The terrain was the same in every direction, vast and rugged with rocks, some cacti and no signs of life. Suddenly a rattlesnake zigzagged across the barren ground, his rattlers emanating a chilling sound. Cari gasped and Reed stopped, slowly backing up, holding his arms out to protect her. The snake wasn't interested in them. He slithered into a crevice.

They inched closer and saw several snakes curled together.

"Oh, God. I hate snakes." Cari turned away with a shudder. "About as much as I hate bats."

"I'm not too fond of them myself." Reed carefully moved on and abruptly stopped again. They both heard it at the same time.

A large rattlesnake lay curled up on a boulder, basking in the warm sun, his rattler making an incessant sound. They were less than three feet away. "Easy," Reed whispered. "Let's just back away."

"Don't move," she whispered back. "Don't even breathe."

They stood perfectly still. The noise of the rattler suddenly ceased.

"Slowly move backward," she instructed, her voice barely audible.

Carefully, they stepped away. When they were out of striking distance, they took off at a run. They kept running until they fell to the ground exhausted.

"What was that about? Are you familiar with rattlesnakes?" Reed asked between gulps of air.

"No." She shuddered again, taking a long breath. "My father took us camping one time when we were visiting a cousin in San Angelo. Cousin Lamar gave us a stern safety lecture before we set off, and I remembered what he said about rattlesnakes." She took another breath. "They have no external ears so they're basically deaf. They're sensitive to vibrations and movement, so if we encountered one, we were told to remain very, very still. That way the snake would not see us as a threat. He said they were very docile creatures. Yeah, right."

Reed shook his head and took several deep breaths. Cari noticed his injury was bleeding, the dark blood vivid against the apple-red scarf.

She sat up. Standing on her knees, she undid the scarf.

"What?" Reed asked.

"You're bleeding again."

"Damn it."

She examined his head and saw the scab had pulled away from the cut. "It's okay. The scab has loosened, probably happened when you hit the ground." She tied the scarf a little tighter and sank down by his side. "Lamar said to never run from a snake."

"Now you tell me."

"I just wanted to get away from that big sucker. Lamar also said they can strike up to two-thirds their length, so once we were a safe distance away my only thought was run like hell."

"The plan worked for me."

She glanced around at the fading light. "It'll be dark soon."

"Yes, and we need a spot to rest."

She wrapped her arms around her waist. "I don't think I can now. There are too many dangers and I'm so thirsty and hungry."

He pushed to his feet. "Don't think about it." He held out his hand and she placed hers into his big one. They were off once again.

As darkness fell, they sank to the ground and rested against a boulder. "Try not to think about the snakes."

"But what else is out there?"

"Try to sleep. Maybe tomorrow we'll make it to the bottom and find help and water." Reed removed his jacket and Cari slipped off the backpack. The air grew chilly and they snuggled under his jacket for warmth. She had dreamed of being held in his arms. But in circumstances very different than this.

She chewed on the inside of her lip. She wasn't the woman he wanted to hold in his arms. Daphne was. On the plane she hadn't wanted to talk about Reed's fiancée, but now she did.

"How did you meet Daphne?"

"It was quite by accident." That soft note in his voice told her that maybe she wasn't ready to talk about his relationship with Daphne after all. Even though the plane crash had given her a new outlook on her feelings for

Reed, her heart was still freshly broken. This was a test she desperately needed, though, to get over Reed. She had to hear all about his love for Daphne. That way she could let go easily. Above everything she wanted him to be happy.

"My mother called all in a panic. She was having a dinner party and dinner parties are her expertise, her talent. She's well known for them. A guest, a friend of my father's and a fellow board member at a bank, called to say his daughter was in town and he and his wife would have to cancel."

"The number-one faux pas is empty chairs at the table. If he and his wife canceled, my mother would be short two guests. If she told him to bring his daughter, she'd have one guest too many. This may sound really petty, but believe me it's very important to my mother."

It did sound petty, but Cari had met Vanessa and understood perfectly.

"She begged me. My father chimed in saying he needed Clyde's vote on a deal at the bank and one dinner wasn't going to hurt me. I held out until the last minute and said I was leaving right after we ate dinner."

"Did you?"

"No. Once I was introduced to Daphne and realized she was as uncomfortable as I was, my whole attitude changed. I took her home and we talked and talked. She didn't expect anything of me and I didn't expect anything of her. We just liked each other and soon we were spending every evening together."

"So she lives in Dallas?"

"She'd just returned from spending the summer in France. She's a ballet dancer and has danced all over the world, but she had grown tired of the travel and wanted to spend some time with her mother and father. I hope she's with them now."

"I'm so damn thirsty," she said just to change the subject, and then she wished she hadn't. It made her realize how thirsty she was.

"Me, too." He shifted into a more comfortable position, stretching his long legs in front of him.

The eerie night sounds surrounded them and Cari didn't want to think about what was out there hiding in the darkness.

"Besides the hunger and thirst, I'm so afraid, I don't think I can sleep."

"I'm exhausted. I know you are, too," Reed

said, looping his arm through hers. "Try to relax."

She was dead tired. All her strength seemed to have drained away. Maybe if she just closed her eyes.

She moved closer to Reed for warmth and comfort and laid her head on his shoulder. His muscles were solid and strong and it gave her the reassurance she needed. Tomorrow help would come and this would just be an unforgettable time in her life. A time she had to face the cold hard facts of survival.

Tomorrow would change her life.

Forever.

The next morning they awoke as the sun rose over the mountains. It was tomorrow and now they had the same issue to face.

Survival.

Without food or water.

Reed flexed his shoulders, dirt and blood stained his clothes as well as his face and hair. He was still attractive to her and all male, especially with that dark growth of beard.

"I could use a cup of coffee," he said, straightening the scarf around his head.

"A mocha frappuccino would be nice." She

gingerly rose to her feet, feeling pain shoot up the back of her legs.

"That's a dessert, not coffee. Coffee is black, strong and a kick in the butt."

She placed her hands on her hips. "I could kick you in the butt if that would help."

He lifted an eyebrow. "You'd enjoy that, wouldn't you?"

She just grinned back.

"I'm your boss, remember?" In one movement he was on his feet, wincing from the pain that must rack his body, too.

She glanced around. "Out here I think we're equals."

His expression changed. "We've always been equals."

"Tell that to Richard Preston."

"Ah." He nodded. "No one is equal to Richard Preston."

"I got that message loud and clear years ago."

"My father is a difficult, complex man. I've had problems dealing with him all my life. So has Marisa."

Cari bent for the backpack on the ground. "He seems very unhappy."

"My father doesn't measure life by happiness."

She slipped on the pack. "By what then?"

"By material things. Success."

"Is that how you judge happiness?" She knew the answer, but she still felt the need to ask.

"Not by a long shot." He tied his jacket around his waist. "My views are so different than my father's. I never planned to spend every waking hour at Dalton's like he had. I took up the reins because it is my heritage. I wanted to prove to my father that success can also be measured by compassion, understanding and fair play. His type of manipulation and control just doesn't work for me."

Something in the sky caught Cari's eye and she looked closer. She pointed. "A plane! Oh my God, it's a plane!" She started running, waving her arms. "We're here. We're here." She tripped and fell headlong into the dirt. Rolling over, she watched it disappear into the clouds. "No! No! No!" she cried.

"It was too far away, Cari." He reached for her hand and pulled her to her feet. "But it was probably a search plane and they'll keep searching."

Cari brushed off her black slacks that were now a shade of filthy brown from the dirt. Her white blouse and jacket were unrecognizable. God, she wanted a bath. And water. Lots of water.

Reed started off and she quickly followed, but she kept her eyes turned to the sky.

Please come back.

Chapter Five

People filled the living room at the Preston home, but there was very little talking. Everyone was waiting.

Richard didn't understand why Marisa had to have the Michaels family here in *his* house. Surely they felt out of place. Sam's children sat around him, rubbing his shoulder or giving him an occasional hug. They seemed close. And annoying.

His wife, Ruth, sat on the sofa, knitting. She said it helped her to stay calm. Vanessa was talking to her as if they were old friends and Ruth was showing his wife how to knit. He had to restrain himself from laughing.

Vanessa evidently was on too much medication.

Marisa sat on the love seat nestled against Colter. His grandchildren, Ellie and Jack, were staying with Tulley, who lived with them. The man had raised Colter and was like a father to him. The kids treated him like a grandfather and that annoyed Richard, too. But it was best the children weren't here.

Thelma served coffee and Richard noticed Sam's hand shook as he took it.

"Daddy, remember that time Cari fell out of the tree?" the younger son, Chase, asked.

"Sure do. I told her a million times not to climb that tree, but she had to prove she could."

"When she got to the top she looked down and froze." Sammy took up the story. "I was on my way up to get her when she lost her balance and fell."

"Right on top of me," Sam said. "I broke her fall." He stared into his cup. "After that she was always scared of heights. I… I… wasn't there to break her fall this time."

"Daddy." Kitty, the younger sister, hugged him. "Cari was always headstrong and independent."

"Yeah. Cari's my middle child, the stubborn one."

"She was determined to conquer her fear of flying and she did." Marisa joined the conversation.

Ruth stopped knitting. "She said she was coming home for Sam's birthday and I was going to make her favorite food, fried chicken, mashed potatoes and gravy."

"You have a close connection to your children," Vanessa remarked. "Sometimes I feel I barely know mine."

"Oh, Vanessa, I'm sorry."

"I am, too. When Reed comes back I'm going to cook him something."

"You don't cook, Vanessa," Richard reminded her.

"Maybe it's time I learned." She glanced at Ruth. "Would you teach me?"

"Sure I will."

"You're losing your mind, Vanessa." He turned and went back to his study. The ring of the phone had him hurrying toward it.

Mr. Avery was on the line and everyone gathered at the door. Richard put the call on speakerphone.

"A plane has located the wreckage. It's on the far side of one of the Davis Mountains.

One wing is clearly visible. We're trying to get a helicopter in there to land, but it's very treacherous. We should have more information shortly."

"Are there any survivors?" Richard asked.

"It's too early to tell. As soon as we get someone on the ground to investigate, we'll know more."

"Thank you, Mr. Avery," Sam said. "We appreciate all that you're doing."

"Things will move quickly now."

"Call the minute you hear anything," Richard said.

"Will do." The phone went dead.

Richard glanced at his guests. "Thelma will serve food while we wait."

"You've been very generous, Mr. Preston," Ruth said. "Thank you."

"Cari works for Dalton's. It's the least I can do."

Ruth nodded and walked out with the rest. Kitty lingered. She looked a lot like Cari with her dark hair and eyes, except she had some sort of streaks in her hair that seemed clownish to him.

"Cari loved working for Dalton's," she told him.

He had no idea why the girl was talking

to him, but he had no choice but to respond. "She's very good at her job."

"Yes. But she's a little afraid of you."

He glanced up. "Really? I always thought Cari Michaels wasn't afraid of anything or anyone."

Kitty looked at the window to the bright blue sky beyond. "I really hope that's true." Tears filled her eyes.

What was he supposed to do? Comfort her? He felt totally helpless and that made him angry. His son was in a plane crash— he didn't feel like dealing with other people's problems right now.

Marisa appeared in the doorway. "Oh, Kitty. I was looking for you." Marisa saw the tears and put her arm around the girl. "Come sit with us. Soon we'll have news."

"I'm so afraid, Marisa."

"I am, too."

Arm in arm they walked out.

Richard stared at the empty space and wondered why his daughter didn't feel a need to comfort him.

By midday Reed and Cari were hot, exhausted and thirsty. The plane had not made another appearance and Reed began to despair of the whole situation. They needed water.

His throat was dry and all he could taste was dust. The scarf tied around his head was beginning to bother him. He removed it and stuffed it into the backpack. He didn't need it anymore.

A jackrabbit jumped out from behind a rock and hopped away.

Cari gasped. "Did you see the ears on that thing?"

"Yeah. Have you noticed we're starting to see more birds and animals?"

"So that means we're close to water?"

"I'm hoping."

Cari removed her lightweight suit jacket. "Is it hotter today?"

Reed stared at her and she followed his gaze to the deep purple bruises on her forearms. "That must have happened in the crash." She probably got them pulling him out of the plane. At that moment he realized she'd risked her life to save his. "You probably have more bruises."

"I'm too tired to look for them." She stretched out on the hard ground and rested her head on her jacket.

Reed stared at her and felt so many things,

but above everything he experienced a deep sense of joy that he knew her and she was in his life. They were both getting weak and they had to have water or food. He had to do something. Suddenly he caught sight of the prickly pear cactus in front of them. They were seeing more cacti, too.

He grabbed the backpack and rummaged through it. "Is there a nail file or something sharp in here?"

"I don't know," she mumbled and he watched her drift into an exhausted sleep. They needed nourishment so he kept searching. He unzipped an inside pocket and found fingernail polish, an emery board and a small metal nail file. Just what he needed.

He moved toward the cactus and carefully plucked away needles. Damn. Needles pierced his fingers but he kept plucking until he had one stem bare. Then he did the same to another and his fingers were beginning to feel like a pincushion. With the file he managed to haphazardly cut the stems from the plant.

Scooting back to Cari, he said, "How about lunch?"

"Make it a double cheeseburger with a super-sized Coke," she murmured. "And lots of ice."

"How about cactus?"

She opened one eye and he wiggled the flat, fat stem in front of her. She sat up immediately. "Where did you get that?"

He pointed to the cactus. "I believe it's a prickly pear. It's a little different than the others we've seen. I've always heard these plants have healing powers, so I'm hoping they're good to eat. Are you game?"

"You bet."

With the file, he split it up the center and pulled the tough skin away to reveal a succulent inside. He tasted it. "Mmm." He licked his lips. "Not bad. It tastes like a cross between green beans and okra. Juicy, but a bit slimy. Of course, my taste buds might be numb from hunger." He handed it to her. "Be careful, there still might be needles. I tried to pull off most of them."

"Wait." He took her hand and rubbed the cactus onto the fading burn and then did the same to the other. "That should help."

"Thank you."

Cari sucked at the cactus greedily. He stopped and watched her. "Oh, this is heavenly."

"I wouldn't call it that." He cut open the other one and took a bite.

"I'm pretending it's ice cream. Homemade peach just the way my mama makes in the summertime when the peaches are ripe."

He stopped eating. "Your mother makes ice cream?"

"Sure. As kids we all took turns cranking the handle on the old ice-cream maker. We were excited when Dad bought her an electric one."

"I don't believe I've ever had homemade ice cream."

"If we get off this mountain, I'll make you some."

Out of the clear blue he wondered if Daphne would make ice cream for him. The thought was insane and he didn't know where it had come from. Daphne didn't need to make him ice cream. She just had to be in his life, sharing the highs and the lows.

But she wasn't.

Cari was.

The sun was hot on his head and he moved uncomfortably, not from the heat but from the thoughts running through his mind. Would Daphne have pulled him from a crashed plane about to burst into flames? Would she have risked her life to save his?

He honestly didn't believe Daphne was that

strong, but he didn't need her to be. She was perfect the way she was.

Cari was different. Her strength and her confidence was always evident in everything she did, from helping Homer conquer his nervousness, to standing up to the board when she thought something was beneficial to Dalton's. She was a fighter, a survivor.

And he was grateful to her for his life.

They continued to eat the cactus and then Reed went back to cut more so they could carry some with them. After a couple of attempts to cut the stem, the file broke.

"Damn it."

"What?"

He held up two pieces of the file. "It's no good now. I can't do anything with these tiny pieces."

"At least we had some nourishment."

He sat down next to her and offered her another piece.

"May I ask you a question?" Cari sat cross-legged and sucked the last juicy bit from the cactus and slowly laid it on the ground.

"Sure. I have all the time in the world."

She licked the remains from her lips and he watched the movement, almost mesmerized.

Looking straight at him, she asked, "Why did you kiss me on the Fourth of July?"

Maybe he didn't have all the time in the world to explain that one. Mainly because he really didn't know.

He shrugged. "The happiness of the day, the moonlight, your beautiful face, I'm not sure."

"And." She snapped her fingers. "Instantly regretted it. I believe you called it a mistake. The sun might be getting to my brain, but I want you to know that hurt my feelings."

He never dreamed he'd hurt her. "I'm sorry. It was just a friendly kiss."

"Yeah, well, what was I going to say after that?"

He frowned at the tone of her voice. "Did you want me to keep kissing you?"

She sprang to her feet, all her tiredness seemed to have disappeared. "I want you to be honest why you did it."

"I am."

"You're a liar, Reed Preston." She struck off down the mountain by herself.

"Cari," he called after her, not having a clue where all this was coming from. One minute she was content eating cactus and the next she was all steamed up about a kiss.

"Cari." He grabbed the backpack, her jacket, and caught up with her. "What are you getting at?"

She turned to face him. "Do you know how long I've been waiting for you to ask me out on a date?"

"What!"

"Do you want me to count the numerous times we worked late and you never suggested going out for a drink? Do you want me to name the endless functions that required a date and you always asked someone else? Do you want me to point out the holidays and birthdays we were invited to and you always made a point of leaving early to make sure everyone knew we weren't a couple? Oh yeah, Reed, you're great for my ego."

He felt the color draining from his face. "I never..."

"That's my point. You never thought of Cari. Never! Yet one evening you suddenly kiss her and act as if you've been branded by fire. And a mere two months later you're madly in love and engaged. Well, congratulations!" She turned and ran, tripped, and her body went rolling down the mountain.

"Cari!" he shouted and half ran and half skidded after her.

She lay on her stomach, so still and life-less. Fear jumped into his throat. He gently turned her over. "Cari, Cari!"

Moaning, she opened her eyes. "Oh." She touched her head and winced.

"Are you okay?"

"I don't know."

"What was in that cactus?"

She made a face. "Truth serum?" She gingerly sat up and glanced down. "Why am I wet?"

Reed noticed the knees of his jeans were wet. The ground was wet.

"I'm sitting in water," Cari said excitedly.

"Yes. There has to be a spring or something close by." He lifted her to her feet. "Cari—"

Her words cut him off. "Let's find the water."

He wanted to talk this out, but water was more important. As he trailed after her he kept thinking about the unexpected kiss.

Why had he kissed her?

Chapter Six

Suddenly there was grass, green grass. Cari knew water had to be close. Pushing back some weeds, she stopped short. A pool lay before her. She blinked. Was it a mirage?

She hurried toward it and fell down, her slacks greedily soaking up the water. Her reflection held her spellbound for a moment. Her hair was glued to her head from sweat. Not a pretty picture. She could care less. Water—life-giving liquid was before her.

Cupping her hands, she dipped them into the water and brought it to her parched lips. She drank her fill and dipped her hands once again.

Swallowing the cool water, she froze. A huge cat appeared on the other side of the pool, growling low in its throat. The tannish-brown fur rose on its back and strength and power was evident in the sleek muscled body.

"It's okay," Reed said in a soothing, soft tone. "Don't move or run. A cat will chase its prey," he whispered to Cari, and then kept talking to the cat, "We pose no threat. It's okay."

The big cat visibly relaxed.

At that moment a deer appeared from the tall grass to drink. The cat immediately bounded after it and the chase was on. Cari looked away, not wanting to see if the cat caught the deer. She just wanted to feast on the water. Even though she was frightened, she desperately needed water. Without it they would die.

She drank her fill while watching the perimeter closely. "It must have been a female."

Reed knelt and cupped his hands, drinking from the pool. He swiped a hand across his mouth and gave her a quizzical look. "Why do you say that?"

"The cat responded to you. All women do."

He sat in the grass and she felt his eyes on

her. "You never did. Or I never thought you did."

She raised her eyes to his. "Forget what I said back there. The sun made me light-headed."

"I think we need to talk about it."

Why had she been so forthright? The words had just come pouring out and she couldn't seem to stop them. She'd said she'd never tell him how she felt, but what if they died out here in the desert? That kept running through her mind. This was really her last chance. The words stuck in her throat, though.

Rejection was strong on her mind and heavy in her chest. She never wanted to ex-perience that kind of pain again. But what did it matter now? They weren't in Dallas. They were alone and might die that way.

"Okay." She plucked a blade of grass and studied it. "I've had a crush on you since the first time I saw you, so you see that makes me just like every other woman."

"You'll never be like every other woman."

They stared at each other for endless sec-onds and something tangible, something real, passed between them. Cari knew they both could feel it.

"You hide it very well," he added.

"Yes. Rule number one—Never let your boss know you're in..." She couldn't finish the sentence.

"In love with him?"

"Maybe." Admitting that out loud might take something stronger than prickly pear cactus followed by a couple of handfuls of water.

"Cari..."

"Like I said, let's forget I lost my mind for a moment."

"I kissed you that night because I wanted to."

Her eyes flew to his, hardly believing he was admitting that. "But you're Marisa's best friend and you work for me. Those two things pulled me back. I don't get involved with anyone who works for me. It's bad for Dalton's and my focus has to always be on Dalton's and its future. If we plunged into an affair, it could not only be detrimental to the company but also to your career. And I know your career is the most important thing to you."

She played with the grass, each word bruising her tired soul.

"The moment I kissed you I realized I was putting Dalton's and your career in jeopardy. I backed off immediately."

Nice to know he had that much willpower. Or that she was less than tempting. She laid the blade in the grass, also looking for somewhere to tuck her pride.

Glancing around, she saw an iridescent green beetle crawling in the grass, and there were big flies around the pool. Every creature out here, big or small, must come here for water. It was the big ones that bothered her. This was not the place to have a chat. Too many dangers.

"We better move on before the cat comes back. What was it anyway?" She was eager to change the subject. The last thing she wanted was to expose her broken heart. Oddly enough, a broken heart was still painful whether you were in Dallas or out in the middle of nowhere fighting to survive.

"Probably a cougar. I heard there were some out here."

They both heard the noise at the same time and turned to see a piglike creature emerge from the grass to drink.

Cari wrinkled her nose. "Oh, heavens, it stinks. That has to be a javelina or is it called a musk hog?"

"I'm not sure. Just be very still," he replied. "With those sharp tusks he could rip us to pieces."

She held her breath as the pig slurped up the water and then quickly darted into the weeds, as eager to get away from them as they were for him to go.

"Cari…"

She could feel Reed's eyes on her and she hurriedly rose to her feet. "We'd better go. Too many wild animals come here for water."

Reed tossed her her jacket and took the empty bottles out of the backpack. "We need to fill these for later." He bent, filled the bottles and handed her one.

She wiggled into the jacket and drank thirstily. So did he. Then he filled the bottles again and stored them in the bag.

"I'd love to dive right in and take a bath," Cari said, giving the water a long look. "But I'm afraid I'd be eaten before I got really wet." She quickly splashed water on her face to wash away some of the grime.

Reed did likewise. "If the cougar missed the deer, he or she—" he lifted an eyebrow at her "—could come back and javelinas usually travel in groups, I've heard, so we better get the hell out of here."

They started off and Cari's legs grew tired,

but she kept going, praying that soon they'd find life other than the very wild species.

The sneakers were hurting her feet, sweat coated her body and the sun burned her skin. The muscles in her legs began to cramp. She ignored the pain, trudging on toward something that seemed as indefinable as Reed's emotions for her. She worked for him. Period. That was it. Or was it? Finally a severe cramp brought her down and she grabbed her aching calf.

Reed knelt beside her. "What is it?"

"Leg cramp." She groaned.

He removed his jacket and placed it on the ground. "Lie down and I'll see if I can massage some of the tightness away."

Don't touch me.

But the pain was so bad she forgot about her pride. "Ah, oh, ah." She moaned as she laid flat or tried to. Her right leg refused to straighten and the cramp kept pulling it tighter.

His hands touched her gently; his fingers and thumbs stroking her calf, rubbing the tight muscle. She closed her eyes and gave herself up to his ministrations. Oh, yeah. This was another one of those moments she'd dreamed about. But again, it was never quite like this.

"Tell me more about your family," he suggested. "Talking might help you to relax."

"Like what?"

"It sounds like you had a happy childhood."

"I never considered my childhood happy. We were poor and had to depend on welfare when my dad's crops would fail." She couldn't believe she'd told him that. Pain was short-circuiting her inhibitions.

"That had to have been hard."

"It was, especially for my dad. He hated that his family had to depend on welfare and that he couldn't give his kids what they wanted."

"What did you want?"

"Brand-new clothes that weren't homemade or hand-me-downs, and shoes that didn't belong to my sister."

"I think most families go through hard times, but there was a lot of love in your house. Right?"

"Yeah." As she watched the twilight fade to darkness, her muscles eased. "Holidays and birthdays were always fun because my mom would cook these scrumptious meals. We all helped, even Sammy and Chase. My dad didn't do much helping in the house except on Mother's Day and my mom's birthday. Those were special days and the rule was it was mom's day and she had to rest."

"Did she?"

"Not for a minute. She said if she's not taking care of her family then she's not doing her job."

"Sounds like a wonderful mother."

"She is." Cari realized her leg wasn't hurting anymore. She sat up. "It's better. You have magic fingers."

He eased down and rested his arms over his knees. "Thank you, ma'am."

She thought turnabout was fair play. "Tell me about your parents."

"Oh, please. You know everything about them."

"I'm talking about your childhood. What was it like as Richard Preston's son?"

Even in the darkness she could see he was thinking. "Lonely."

She hadn't expected that response. "Lonely?"

"That's about the only way to describe it. I had to be immaculately dressed at all times. I had dinner with my parents about three times a week. The other times I ate alone in the dining room. I was allowed outside to play four times a week, but I wasn't allowed to go to a public park. That was my dream as a kid—to play in a park like a normal kid. My dad said I wasn't like other kids. I was a Preston and I had to act accordingly. All I knew was that I was a kid and wanted to play."

Cari thought that was sad and she wanted to hug him, but she didn't.

"When Marisa was born, I was the happiest kid on the planet. I had a sister, someone to play with. I was five years older but it didn't seem to matter. I watched over her. I'd sneak to her room and just watch her sleep. When she was older, I'd read to her until she fell asleep." His voice grew soft and she knew how much he loved his sister.

Then his voice changed and she felt him stiffen beside her. "Our holidays were nothing like yours. At Christmas I opened presents alone with a nanny. My father was always in his study making deals and my mother was still asleep. At Christmas dinner I'd excitedly show them my gifts, but they weren't interested. It was nice having Marisa to open gifts with and to share the excitement of the holiday." He stopped for a moment.

"When my mother left my father and took Marisa to New York to live, I was heartbroken. I cried myself to sleep for weeks and my world got lonelier."

"Your mother didn't take you?" She already knew this, but still couldn't keep the shock out of her voice.

"No. It was in the agreement they made. I stayed with my father and Marisa went with Vanessa. After that I ate alone in my room. I didn't even want to go to the dining room. My dad was always busy or out with a lady friend. When I was twelve he sent me to Arizona to a private school. I didn't know a soul and the world seemed a very big and lonely place."

She rubbed his arm, needing to touch him. His hand covered hers and she could literally feel his sadness, his loneliness. Her heart broke a little more for the boy who had everything and yet had nothing.

She squeezed his arm and tried to lighten the conversation. "My homemade clothes and welfare is beginning to look really good."

"Because your family had love. The Preston family had very little of that."

Cari thought of what Richard and Vanessa had done to Marisa and her baby because Marisa had fallen in love with the wrong man. They were ruthless and heartless and had paid dearly for that.

"Your parents almost lost Marisa because of their manipulation, but they tried to make amends and were truly sorry. For them to do that and for Marisa to forgive them, there has to be love. A little different than normal, perhaps, but still love."

"Yes." He ran his hands over his face. "It's definitely different. Look." He pointed to the sky. "A shooting star."

"Or, we could be close to Marfa, known for its mysterious lights."

"Maybe." He turned to her. "How's your leg?"

"Much better," she replied, still feeling his fingers on her skin.

"We better find a spot to bed down for the night."

Cari glanced around at the darkness. "I vote we stay right here. Anything could be out there." She trembled. "Why didn't the plane come back? Why isn't someone searching for us?"

"They probably found the wreckage."

"Oh." It finally dawned on her. "They think..."

"We all perished in the crash."

Cari wrapped her arms around her waist. "We're going to die out here, aren't we?"

"Not if we keep going." He scooted closer to her and picked up his jacket. "Do you want to lie on it or use it for cover?"

"Cover, I suppose."

They lay down on the hard, dusty ground and Reed placed his jacket over them. She snuggled into his chest as if she'd been doing it all her life. So natural. So right.

"I missed my dad's birthday," she murmured.

"I don't think he's worried about that."

"I know. I hope we find someone tomorrow who can get word to them." As it grew chilly, Cari snuggled closer. "Do you think your parents are worried?"

"Yes, in their own way."

"Did you always attend private school?"

"Until I went to the University of Texas."

"Then you started to party and have fun."

"Well." She could feel him smiling. "I'm told that's what I was born to do?"

"And you do it very well."

For a moment there was nothing but silence.

"I'm sorry I hurt you."

She didn't have to ask what he was talking about because she knew. *The kiss.*

She took a long breath. "I'm glad you found someone who will make you happy, someone who will fill that loneliness in you." It surprised her that she meant it. She wanted him to be happy even if it was with Daphne.

"That seems so far away."

"It feels like we're in a world all our own."

"It's almost preferable to my world. All my life something has been expected of me—to be immaculate, patient, understanding, proper, intelligent and to take up the Preston reins of Dalton's. My whole life has been geared toward perfection and performance. Dalton's was the ultimate goal."

"And you've achieved it."

He was quiet for a moment and she turned slightly to look at him. "What?" she asked quietly.

"Out here where life is as real as it can get I'm wondering if it was *my* goal or my father's. Or if I know the difference."

"Oh, Reed." Unable to resist, she touched his face, his growth of beard sending a tingly sensation down her arm. "Since you've been at the helm of Dalton's, the profits have been at an all-time high. People like working for you and they do their best. I hate to use an old cliché but you were born for the job."

"But I'm still asking myself if it's what I want to do for the rest of my life. I'm thirty-six and I'm still asking myself that question."

"Why do you think that is?"

He rubbed his face against her hand. "Because I know my father is still manipulating things behind the scenes. I can't prove it yet, but once I do I know I'll be gone for good."

Her heart skipped a beat. "Will leaving Dalton's make you happy?"

"Like my father, I'm not sure I know what happiness is."

Something in the tone of his voice and the lonely picture he'd painted of his childhood gave her the courage to gently touch her lips to his.

His mouth covered hers instantly and she wrapped her arms around him, enjoying this time out of time. The kiss went on as each gave and took what they needed.

The cold, hard ground was beneath their dirty and sweaty bodies. Danger lurked just beyond in the darkness, but the moment his lips touched hers she was in heaven, floating on a cloud.

He rested his forehead against hers, his

wisps of breath like an iridescent flame warming her in the most sensual way.

"Cari…"

"Shh." She didn't want to break the illusion that he cared something for her.

"I'm engaged to someone else."

Her heart twisted. "I know."

And she didn't expect one thing from him, except this moment.

It belonged to her.

Chapter Seven

Richard quickly showered and went downstairs. He heard voices coming from the dining room and knew his guests were having breakfast. Thank God they hadn't brought their kids and spouses. It was ridiculous they were here in the first place. In what way was this helping his son?

Thelma appeared in the doorway. "Can I get you anything, sir?"

"Coffee and a couple of those sweet rolls the cook makes."

"Yes, sir."

"I suppose our guests are gorging themselves."

"No, sir. They've barely touched the food. They're just drinking coffee."

"Why the hell not? It's free."

Thelma nervously edged toward the door. "It's not about the food. They're worried and upset."

As the maid left, Richard sank into his chair. Why couldn't they all get the hell out of his house and leave him alone. He was worried and upset, too. But no one seemed to notice. Or care.

"Why was Thelma in such a hurry?" Marisa asked as she walked in.

"Who knows?"

"Don't you think we should have heard something by now?" She brushed back her blond hair, looking so beautiful and as delicate as a flower. His daughter. Her inner strength always surprised him. It also maddened him at times.

"We should hear something soon," he told her.

"We have to. This is taking a toll on all of us." Her honey-colored eyes looked so sad and he wanted to comfort her, to tell her Reed would soon walk through the door. For some reason he couldn't do either of those things.

"Richard," Vanessa called from the doorway. "Why don't you phone Mr. Avery. They've had plenty of time to get someone on the ground to investigate. We need to know what happened to our children. We need to know they're okay."

His fragile wife was growing stronger during this crisis instead of weaker. He expected her to stay in bed with a sedative, but she was playing hostess to the utmost of her abilities.

Before Richard could answer his wife, the doorbell rang. They hurried into the living room as Winston ushered Mr. Avery in. At his solemn face, Richard knew the news wasn't good.

"I'm sorry," Mr. Avery said. "I wanted to tell you in person." He paused. "There are no survivors."

"Oh," Marisa cried and almost crumpled to the floor, but Colter caught her. He swung her up into his arms and carried her upstairs.

Ruth began to sob uncontrollably and Sam just held her as their children gathered around them.

Richard glanced at Vanessa's shattered expression and thought they should be comforting each other like the Michaels family were. But they were lost somewhere within their own grief. Their son, a child they had created together, was gone and they didn't know how to accept that. How to live with that reality.

Ruth walked over to Vanessa. "I'm so sorry."

Vanessa clung to her and they cried for the children they would never see again.

Sam rubbed his wife's back, his eyes full of tears. "Let's go home, Mother. We have to make arrangements for our girl." He looked at Mr. Avery. "When will they bring the bodies in?"

Mr. Avery swallowed. "We're not sure if it was on impact or after they'd crashed, but the plane exploded. The investigating team will carefully sift through the remains."

"Oh." Sam's knees seemed to buckle and Sammy and Chase were there to hold him up.

"There's nothing left of our girl?" Ruth wiped away tears.

Mr. Avery shook his head. "I'm afraid not. I'm sorry."

"Oh, my. Oh, my." Judith and Kitty led Ruth to a sofa.

The room became painfully quiet, interspersed with sobs.

"The team should be able to identify human remains and they are already there setting up to work, but as I said, the terrain is very treacherous and the investigation will go slowly. I will keep you apprised of the situation." He inclined his head toward Richard. "I'm so sorry for your loss."

At that moment Daphne rushed in. "Has there been any news?" she asked eagerly.

Richard went to her, not sure how to tell her. "Mr. Avery just told us there are no survivors."

"What?" Her skin turned a pasty white and Richard guided her to a chair.

"That can't be true," she mumbled. "We're planning to get married. I met yesterday with an architect to go over the plans for our house." She reached into her purse for a handkerchief and dabbed at her eyes. "This can't be true."

Kitty knelt by her chair and patted her hands. "It's true. My sister was on the plane, too."

"Who's your sister?"

"Cari Michaels."

"Yes. I met her the other day. A nice young woman."

"The very best," Kitty replied.

Daphne stuffed the handkerchief back into her purse. "I have to tell my parents. They'll be so upset. We'll have to cancel all the arrangements for the wedding. This can't be happening." Daphne began to cry and Kitty hugged her. "I can't go on without Reed."

Richard took over and helped Daphne to her feet. "I'll get you a driver. You're in no condition to be behind the wheel."

"Thank you. I am feeling a little confused."

"I'll call your parents so they'll know you're on the way." Winston helped Daphne to the door.

Richard went into his study and slammed the door. His son. His only son was dead and there was no one to comfort him. He had his big company, his big house, his big bank accounts, but now they brought him very little comfort.

Sitting down, he choked back the sobs in his throat. He could always control and manipulate life to his advantage and he had done it regardless of anyone's feelings. Suddenly he felt the price of that heavy on his heart.

His son was gone.

Nothing in the world could bring him back. For the first time in Richard's life he felt powerless and helpless. Unable to deal with his thoughts, he hurried back to the living room.

Sam was talking. "Ruth, it's time for us to

go home. The Prestons have put up with us long enough."

"Yes, you're right." Ruth wiped away her tears. "I hate to go without knowing how Marisa is. Cari wouldn't want her to be sad."

Vanessa rose and stumbled, grabbing the sofa for support. "I'll check on my daughter, but right now I can't seem to move my feet."

Judith was immediately at her side. "Sit down, Mrs. Preston. We've all just received a terrible shock."

"I need to go to my daughter."

They heard a noise and Marisa and Colter entered the room. Marisa's eyes were red and swollen, her hair damp from her tears. She went into Vanessa's arms and they hugged, then she hugged Ruth and they sat side by side on the sofa.

"Cari and Reed were my best friends. When they were in a room together you could feel the energy between them. I always thought they should be together." Marisa hiccuped. "Now they are."

"I missed so much of Reed's life," Vanessa said. "I guess I'll never get over that. A boy should be with his mother, but sadly I wasn't a very good mother." She brushed at her tears. "I never cooked for him."

Ruth hugged Vanessa. "You did your best."

"Cari was my adventurous child," Sam spoke up, his hands folded between his legs. "She was always dreaming big dreams. I tried to discourage her because I didn't want her to get hurt, but sometimes a father has to let go. When she was eighteen and left for Dallas, I didn't sleep for a week. So many times I wanted to go and get her, make her come home and marry Will down the road. He was crazy about her." He sighed. "That was my dream, not hers. With hard work she made her dream come true. She died doing what she loved. Some time in the near future I hope I find some peace in that."

Richard had heard enough. He walked into his study and slammed the door again. Plopping into his chair, he stared out the window to the bright sunny September day. But the sun had just gone out in his world.

Sam Michaels was an idiot. Why would he let an eighteen-year-old girl come to Dallas? He should have forced her...

Like Richard had forced Marisa.

He thought back to that trying time. Marisa was seventeen and pregnant by a rodeo cowboy she'd met in Vegas. She had such a brilliant future ahead of her as a concert pianist. She was so talented.

That was Richard and Vanessa's dream.

Marisa's had been entirely different.

Through manipulation Richard had ruined his daughter's life. But Marisa was happy now. Living her dream.

Maybe Sam wasn't such an idiot.

His children trusted him. Loved him.

Richard's relationship with his children was more businesslike than loving. That's all he knew how to do—run a business. Being raised by a less-than-friendly uncle, Richard never knew much about love. He thought happiness came with wealth and that's the reason he went after Vanessa Dalton the moment he set eyes on her. He intended to own Dalton's one day. And he did.

Then why wasn't he happy?

His son was gone.

A pain pierced his chest as sharp as a knife. He took a deep breath and a tear rolled from his eye. *His only son was dead.* Another tear followed.

After a slight knock at the door, the girl Kitty came in. "Mr. Preston, my parents are getting ready to—" She stopped when she saw his tears. "I'm so sorry." Then she did something no one else had done during this whole ordeal. She hugged him, a real hearty hug that reached his soul.

His arms lay heavy in his lap though. He didn't have the ability to hug her back.

She knelt in front of him. "Why don't you join us in the living room. We're telling stories about Cari and Reed. I bet you have a lot of stories about Reed."

"I don't feel like talking."

"Then just come and be with your wife and daughter."

"I'd rather be alone."

She stood and glanced out the window. "I hope you were right about what you said earlier."

"What was that?"

"That Cari wasn't afraid of anything."

"She was a strong woman and stood up to men three times her size."

"Did she ever stand up to you?"

"Oh, yeah. She invaded a lot of board meetings when things weren't going the way she thought they should. I almost had her thrown out one time."

"Why didn't you?"

"Reed stopped me. He said he was CEO and he agreed with Cari. You see, we have five stores in Dallas and the board was voting to close one that had low profits."

"Cari wanted to keep the store open?"

"Yes. She said it needed updating and revamping. The store was one of the older ones and we hadn't done anything to it in years."

"What happened?"

"We voted the way she wanted."

"Wow. She had that much power."

"Reed backed her and that did it."

"But you're Richard Preston. Surely you could have influenced the board to vote your way."

"Maybe, but I didn't push it. My son was fighting to make his mark and I decided to back off."

"Because you loved him."

No. I wanted the venture to fail so he could see what a flake Cari was. He didn't tell Kitty that, though. It was even harder to admit that to himself. He had been set on proving to Reed that Cari did not deserve to be vice president.

"So what happened?"

He brushed a hand across his eyes. "After the remodeling, the store showed a profit in the first year. It hasn't stopped."

"So Cari and Reed were right?"

Richard frowned. Why was he talking to this insipid little hairdresser? Because she was the only one who had showed him any compassion. Not that he deserved it. "What does it matter? They're both gone."

"They'll live on forever through us."

"Please, just leave me alone."

She looked at him for a moment, her eyes so like Cari's. "My parents are getting ready to leave and we'd like to thank you for your hospitality."

"Whatever." He dismissed her with a wave of his hand.

"Goodbye, Mr. Preston. I hope one day you'll be able to say you love your son." After that, she walked out.

He stared after her. Could she read his mind?

It wasn't that he couldn't say it. He didn't deserve Reed's love. He'd manipulated him just as he'd manipulated Marisa. Now Richard was going to have to live with that for the rest of his life.

He'd promised to stay out of their lives and to not interfere. He'd lied. Reed had his whole life ahead of him and Richard had to make sure he made the right choices, especially in a wife.

Daphne was Richard's choice for Reed. From the moment he'd met her, *he'd* known she'd make Reed a perfect wife. So he and his friend set up the meeting—even Vanessa hadn't known. He could always count on Vanessa to cause a scene if anything disturbed her dinner party. A little coaxing and she'd called Reed immediately.

Everything had fallen into place.

Now it was over.

Nothing exposed the truth more than a plane crashing in the middle of nowhere without a warning. For the first time Richard realized he was being punished. It was time to pay the piper for his manipulations. And the piper took everything he treasured.

It took his son.

Chapter Eight

The morning dawned just like the others—with the sun rising to beat down on the desolate landscape. Cari sat up and stretched every aching muscle in her body. Her clothes were filthy and her body grimy. She yearned for food, water and a hot bath. And civilization. And more water. God, she was so thirsty.

Reed rose to his feet with a groan. "Damn, sleeping on the ground is hell." He had a full growth of beard and it looked rugged and sexy. It had felt the same way last night as he'd rubbed it against her face. She still felt the evocative caress.

I'm engaged to someone else came back to her.

Any other time those words would have hurt, but out here where they were struggling to survive they didn't seem to matter.

A big lizard ran across the ground in front of her. She didn't even flinch. Lizards were a familiar sight, as were ants, and she'd grown accustomed to seeing them. She flexed her shoulders. "Well, Junior, what's the plan for the day?"

The corner of his mouth twitched. "Glad to see you still have your sense of humor."

"It's about all I have left."

And my pride.

His eyes clung to hers. "About last night..."

She shrugged, getting to her feet. "No big deal. I've been kissed before and hopefully will be again."

He picked up his jacket, shook it out and tied it around his waist. "I just don't want to mislead you. I love Daphne and if I ever get out of here I'm going to marry her."

Cari looked up at the bright blue sky and its endless depth. Under God's umbrella it was hard to keep her feelings bottled up. And there was something about the way he'd said the words, as if he'd rehearsed them many times. Under His mighty blue sky she said to hell with it. She wasn't keeping her feelings buried like a secret treasure anymore.

She stared directly at him. "Are you sure you love her?"

He frowned. "Of course."

"You want me to tell you what I think?"

His eyes darkened. "No. Not really."

"I'm going to tell you anyway."

"Cari..."

Nothing could stop her now. Not the fear of rejection. Not her job security. Nothing.

"When we shared that brief kiss on the Fourth, I think it scared the hell out of you. You felt the spark and immediately denied it. Not Cari, she's Marisa's friend and she works for me. That's bull. So what if I'm Marisa's friend and I work for the company? Big deal. We're adults and can handle whatever happens. But you searched for damage control and found it in Daphne Harwood."

His eyes glowed with anger. "That's not true."

"Last night you didn't kiss me like a man in love with someone else."

He didn't say anything and his silence was fuel for everything building inside her.

"I'll go a step further and tell you the truth

the way it appears to me. Daphne was hand-picked by your father."

"That's a lie," he said, anger now evident in his voice.

She didn't even pause. "She's a wealthy socialite with an accomplished dancing background. Does that ring any bells, Reed? Daphne's a carbon copy of your mother." She drew in deeply. "A woman you would avoid just on principle, but you embraced her completely. Why? I keep asking myself."

"Why?" he asked with a note of sarcasm. "You seem to have all the answers."

"Because you're scared," she shot back. "You're scared of all those feelings that have been developing between us. You're scared of love." Her voice suddenly softened. "Maybe it has something to do with your childhood and you're happier with a woman who can't touch your emotions. Maybe you're happier letting your father pull the strings that dictate your life. It's easier that way."

"You have it all wrong. You're talking out of hurt pride."

She waved a hand. "Oh, I'm talking out of a lot more than hurt pride. I'm talking honestly. I'll tell you about hurt pride. When I was eighteen, I was stood up for the prom because I wasn't a part of the 'in crowd'." She made quotes with her fingers. "I sat in my parents' living room in my homemade gown and my sister's shoes I had stuffed with tissues feeling a pain like I'd never felt before. I vowed then no one would ever treat me that way again."

She paused. "For years I've thought of you as the Prince of Dalton's, and in my heart you had a kind of shine that never could be tarnished. Reality has a way of opening eyes and mine are wide open. I was happy living with a fantasy, but the truth is there is no razzle-dazzle Reed Preston. He's just a man who's scared to take a chance, a chance on love. Just don't use excuses like I work for you. Be honest and tell it like it is." She turned away. "Now I'm going to walk my way out of here if it's the last thing I do."

Reed stared after her, rooted to the spot as so many painful emotions chugged through him. He loved Daphne. He loved… Then why couldn't he remember her kiss, her touch? All he could feel was Cari.

Her words were like the needles of the cactus, sharp and pointed, piercing him. Pulling away wasn't an option. He had to feel the pain and deal with it.

He had to be honest.

Working with Cari was stimulating and a challenge. That's the reason he'd appointed her as vice president. She had a spark and vitality that brightened his job at Dalton's. She knew the store from the ground up and she had a good relationship with the executives and the staff. Everyone liked her and admired her.

So did he.

Sinking to the ground, he tried to come to grips with the truth. He took a deep breath that came from the bottom of his lungs. *He'd wanted to kiss Cari—for a long time*. The truth of that was as barbed as the cactus and maybe as healing as its powers.

He was afraid, just as she'd said. It was safer being alone and emotionally detached. That way no one could hurt him. What about Daphne? His feelings for her were real or at least he'd thought they were.

Staring at the barren ground, rocks, sparse grass and cacti, he decided this had to be purgatory or hell. His penance was the truth. He felt the sun on his head and knew he was right. Only the very tough survived here. How tough was he? Was he tough enough to admit the truth? His father was manipulating his life—what was he going to do about it?

He stood and watched Cari's receding back. First, he had to talk to her. Maybe somewhere out here he could salvage his pride, his strength and his character.

Once he had that in place he would know what the rest of his life would be like.

He prayed he had one.

Cari walked on, regretting she'd lost her temper. The truth had a way of opening wounds that could never be healed. Working with Reed was now going to be impossible. It would be tense and stressful. That is, if they ever got out of this place.

Voices carried on the sultry wind. She stopped, frantically glancing around and then she saw the puffs of smoke. A campfire! She ran toward it.

As she reached the perimeter, two Mexican boys about eighteen jumped to their feet, quickly brandishing switchblades. The sun glistened off the sharp steel.

Her breath stalled in her throat. "Help. We need help," she managed to say.

They didn't respond and fear tiptoed across her skin. One boy eyed her up and down and walked toward her, the knife held tightly in his hand. *"Ay, una señorita muy bonita."*

In an instant Cari realized they were illegals from Mexico hiding out as they made their way into Texas. They didn't look friendly. They looked scared and dangerous.

"We need help, please," she said again, hoping to make them understand. "Our plane crashed."

One boy grinned, displaying yellow teeth, and reached for her arm. She jerked away. Before she knew it, the other boy was on her and she fought with all her strength.

"Let her go," Reed shouted, and the boys immediately paused and pointed their knives at Reed.

"Alto, Señor," one boy ordered as Reed advanced.

"Listen," Reed said, his voice coaxing. "We've been in a plane crash and we're looking for a town or someplace to make a phone call. We mean you no harm."

The boys glanced at each other. One still held tightly to Cari. *"No hablo inglés."*

Reed walked closer just as the other boy reached out and hit him with his fist. Reed went down.

The boys grabbed Cari and ran. She struggled and that slowed them down. But the two youths were surprisingly strong. She didn't want to think what they wanted with her.

"Let me go," she kept screaming, kicking and fighting every way she could. Their breaths smelled like burned baked beans. Her nightmare had suddenly turned into a mega nightmare. She prayed Reed was okay.

Reed rolled to his feet in a heartbeat, rubbing his jaw. Cari! He had to find Cari. The sun seemed to blink and fade and he fought to stay conscious. He couldn't pass out. Cari was in danger.

Staring at the ground, he saw the ruts, and it was very evident Cari was dragging her feet. That made them easier to track. He didn't even know he had the skill. He had to stop a couple of times to regain his balance.

On and on he followed the trail, the heat and dust suffocating. About an hour later he came upon them. He crawled on his belly over dried grasses and rocks, avoiding the cacti, so he could get closer and listen without being detected.

The two boys were conversing.

"Qué se vaya. Ella no vale la pena."

"Me gusta mucho la señorita. Es muy bonita."

"Ellos van a atrapamos."

"Cobarde."

"Bastardo. No voy a regresar a México."

Reed glanced up to check their location. The two guys were deep in conversation, or in deep dispute. He spoke some Spanish and was going to try to talk with them when the boy had hit him. They were arguing about whether to let Cari go or not. One thought she was pretty and the other was afraid of being caught. He didn't want to go back to Mexico. The other called him a coward.

Cari sat to the side, her arms folded across her knees and her face buried on them. She seemed spent and exhausted.

He inched slowly forward until he was within her line of vision. *Raise your head, Cari.* She remained hunched over. Suddenly the bigger guy pushed the smaller one and a fight was on. The small one tackled him and they went down fighting, dust swirled around them.

Cari looked up and Reed quickly stood, motioning for her to run. She sprinted toward him. He grabbed her hand and they were off, running for their lives. Curses followed them and they kept going, over bare ground, rocks and cacti. The curses faded, but they didn't stop until they fell down.

They lay prone for several minutes. Reed's breath came in gasps and his chest hurt, but he held tight to Cari's hand.

"Are you okay?" he asked between deep breaths.

She nodded her head and he knew she was unable to speak.

After a few more minutes, he sat up and removed the backpack. He fished out the last bottle of water and waited for her to regain her strength.

"Cari," he whispered.

She rolled over and he helped her to sit up. He held up the bottle and she grabbed it, drinking thirstily. When she'd drunk half, she handed it back. He shook his head.

"Drink it all. You need it." In that moment all his confused thoughts became crystal clear. He'd give his life to save hers. It was a startling revelation and it solidified everything she'd said about him.

He'd been fighting his attraction for her because she threatened to touch his heart. That private part of him that was open to no one.

She gave a half smile. "Ah, my knight in shining armor."

"You bet. Razzle-dazzle Reed Preston."

She grimaced. "I'm sorry I said all those nasty things."

He shrugged. "Sometimes the truth is nasty."

She held out the bottle. "Take it. You might have to carry me out of here."

Taking the water, he screwed the lid tight and placed it back in the bag. She would need it later.

She trembled and was unable to stop. He gathered her close and held her. "You're safe now," he whispered against her sweat-coated hair. "You're safe."

She drew back and wiped at her dirt-stained face. "But for how long? I thought once we met a person they would help us. Not...not..."

"Shh. We just met the wrong people. I'm sure they're trying to get as far away as possible now."

She shuddered. "I hope so." Suddenly she laid her head in his lap. "I'm so tired."

"Try to sleep and then we'll walk on." He wouldn't close his eyes in case he was wrong and the Mexicans tried to find them.

"Reed."

"Hmm?"

"Are we going to make it home?"

"Yes," he replied. "We just encountered two people and soon we'll encounter more. We just have to keep going."

"I wonder how my parents are."

"They'll be better once they know you're alive."

"I don't want Marisa to be sad."

"My sister is very strong." He stroked Cari's hair. "I'm sorry that idiot stood you up for the prom. That had to have been awful for a young girl."

She raised her head. "Yes, it was, but I went anyway."

He lifted an eyebrow. "You did? How did that happen?"

She sat up. "Well, in high school I dated one of the rich, popular boys, Jared Cramer. I was excited about the prom that was coming up. We had talked about it. I couldn't believe I was going with 'Mr. Cool.' That's what the girls called him."

"Mr. Cool didn't show up?" he asked when she stopped and stared at the ground.

"No." Her dark eyes held a faraway look. "Like I said, I sat in my parents' living room and waited. Finally I called Jared and he laughed. He said he was just joking. His parents would die if he took me. I wasn't from their circle of friends. He added I wouldn't enjoy the prom anyway and he'd see me in school."

"Did you still date 'Mr. Jerk'?"

"Are you kidding?" The fire was back in her eyes. "I was crushed and planned to cry myself to sleep, but my mother was angry her daughter had been treated so callously. She said I was going to the dance and when I saw the tears in her eyes, I knew I'd do anything she wanted to make that look go away. Will Dunbar lived down the road from us and he wasn't exactly in with the 'in crowd' either. My mother called his mother and before we knew it we were on the way to the prom."

"No one but Cari Michaels has that much nerve or confidence," he said, grinning. "Did you have a good time?"

"You bet." A tentative smile touched her lips. "We did all the crazy dances and laughed most of the night. Jared tried to talk to me, but I ignored him." She picked up a rock and turned it over and over in her hand. "As a kid I used to love shiny, sparkly things I saw in Wal-Mart. When my mom would buy me the shiny bauble, the shine never lasted. Once the shine was gone, I was left with a piece of junk. That's how I saw Jared that night. All his shine was gone and what was left wasn't attractive or appealing anymore."

For a moment there was total silence and he could actually feel her pain of long ago. He admired her strength and courage and hated that she'd been hurt so cruelly. "You're incredible."

"Or stupid. I dredged up the courage to go to make my mom happy."

"Did it make you happy?"

"Yes. It proved to me that no one can make me feel bad unless I let them. I decided right then and there that no one was ever going to make me feel less of a person again."

He brushed hair from her forehead. "Not even me, huh?"

Her eyes met his. "Not even you, razzle-dazzle man."

He cupped her face. "You're right about me. I'm afraid, and all my choices have stemmed from that fear. You grew up surrounded by love, but I've had very little of that. It's hard for me to open up that side of me." He realized he was doing it now and it felt right and easy with Cari.

"You're being honest and that's a start."

He swallowed. "When we get back, I have

to sort out my relationship with Daphne. I have to find out if my father set up our meeting. I can see now it's a very real possibility."

His thumb made a circle on her cheek. "I do have strong feelings for you, but I can't do anything about them until I straighten out my life. I have to do this right."

Her eyes sparkled. "Would it be wrong to kiss you?"

He touched her lips gently, tasting dirt and sweat, but all he could feel was her warmth, her inner strength. Blood pounded in his veins and his tired body never felt more alive. "You're everything that's right in my world."

She curled her arms around his neck and they held on to each other for this moment in time.

It was all they had.

It was all they needed.

Chapter Nine

Richard sat in his study with the door locked, a bottle of bourbon in front of him. Untouched. He kept staring at it, knowing solace and forgetfulness were within.

But he had to remember.

Everything.

He twisted the bottle. Marisa, Colter and the kids were in the kitchen with Vanessa, making cookies. Craziest idea he'd ever heard of. Vanessa wanted to make something for Reed when he returned. She had decided Reed wasn't dead. Richard supposed it was the only way she could cope and he didn't have the energy to make her see the truth. Evidently Marisa didn't either because she went along with the insane plan and had even tried coaxing him into joining them. He wasn't in the mood for company, though. Not even his grandchildren's.

Marisa said they needed to be together, so the whole family was spending the night. He didn't think the kids needed to be told yet, but Marisa and Colter had felt otherwise. Now they were in the kitchen talking and sharing.

As the Michaelses had. Thank God they had finally gone home. But Richard still didn't have any peace.

A tap sounded at the door.

"Go away!" he shouted.

"I just wanted to know if you needed anything, sir," Winston asked, his voice muffled.

Richard jumped up, marched to the door and yanked it open. "Yes, Winston. I would like to be left alone. Do you understand me?"

"Yes, sir."

Thirteen-year-old Ellie strolled into the room. She was a blond beauty, a replica of her mother, except she had her father's green eyes.

"Mommy sent me to get you, Grandpa." She linked her arm through his. "You have to be with family. Grandma is cooking and it's a sight to see. Uncle Reed would be freaked out—I sure am."

He went with her like a dutiful puppy. She should hate him for what he'd stolen from her—her mother. It had taken eight years for Marisa to discover her daughter was alive and living with her father. But Ellie had a forgiving soul and a loving heart. Richard had Colter to thank for that.

He never had, though.

As they entered the big kitchen, he saw Colter and Jack, his four-year-old grandson, sitting on bar stools at the granite countertop island.

Marisa and Vanessa stared at something in a bowl. No servants were around, so Vanessa must have dismissed them.

"Now cream the eggs and sugar," Marisa told her mother.

"Hi, Grandpa." Jack raised a hand. "Grandma is making sugar cookies for Uncle Reed and we're going to decorate them. Right, Daddy?"

Colter put an arm around Jack. "Right, son."

"Do you mean add cream?" Vanessa asked, her linen pantsuit covered with a white apron.

"No, Mother," Marisa answered in a patient

voice. "You beat them together until the mixture is creamy."

"What do I beat it with?"

Good grief. He was surprised Vanessa had even found the kitchen. He rolled up his shirtsleeves. "This is how you do it." He picked up a spoon and whipped the ingredients until the mixture was creamy. He remembered doing this as a kid at his uncle's during the holidays. He'd forgotten that. "That's it." He sat the bowl aside.

Vanessa clapped her hands. "Oh, Richard. I didn't know you could do that."

"Grandpa can do anything," Ellie said, leaning against Colter. "Just like my daddy."

Richard winked at her. "Now we add the rest of the ingredients." He was getting into it. Soon he and Vanessa were cutting out cookies. Ellie and Jack added sprinkles, chocolate shavings and M&Ms. Marisa popped them into the oven and then they waited, sitting around the island.

"Uncle Reed would be proud," Ellie said.

"Yes, he would," Marisa added. "He'd want us to be together as a family."

"Have you talked to Ruth or any of the Michaels family?" Vanessa asked.

"I talked to Ruth this morning and they're

waiting a few days before they make arrangements. She said they needed some time and they wanted to wait until the investigation was finished."

"Mommy, are the cookies ready?" Jack asked.

The oven dinged. "Yes." Marisa went to get them while Vanessa brought glasses and milk.

"I want an M&M one." Jack propped himself up on his knees looking at the cookies.

"We have to say a prayer," Ellie said. "We have to hold hands, too." They gathered close to the island. Richard looked into Vanessa's eyes and she smiled. It warmed his cold heart. He took her hand and reached for Marisa's. The others joined in.

"Who's going to say the prayer?" Ellie asked.

"You can, sweetie," Marisa replied.

"Okay." They bowed their heads. "Dear God, we miss Uncle Reed and Cari, but we're happy they're with you. Please help us not to be sad. And please bless this food. Amen."

No one moved or said anything for a solid minute. They were linked by hands, by family and by blood and no one wanted to let go.

Finally they moved to their stools, each dealing with their own sadness.

They ate in a comfortable silence. Halfway through his cookies, Jack's eyelids began to droop.

"Time for bed." Colter gathered up his son.

Marisa stood. "I'll be back to help with the dishes."

"Darling, no." Vanessa hugged and kissed her. "I'll take care of the dishes. Put your babies to bed."

Ellie frowned. "Grandma, I'm not a baby."

"Pardon me, young lady."

Ellie hugged them and followed her parents.

Richard and Vanessa were left alone in an intolerable silence.

"I need to put some of these up for Reed." Vanessa grabbed a plate and plastic wrap. "I want them to be fresh."

Richard watched her nervous movements and knew he had to say something. She had to face the truth. "Vanessa, Reed is—"

"Don't say it," she snapped and carried the cookies to the refrigerator.

"Vanessa." He tried again.

She hurriedly carried plates to the sink, ignoring him. Opening the dishwasher, she started to stack dishes inside. He didn't even know she knew how to do that. Once she had the dishes done, she wiped the counter.

He took her hands and led her to a stool. "We need to talk."

"I know what you're going to say and I don't want to hear it. Let me deal with this in my own way."

"Okay." He nodded. "Believe what you want, but I have to tell you something else." He had to tell someone or it was going to eat him alive. Sharing wasn't big on his list of favorite things, but it was the only way he was going to find any measure of peace.

"Richard, please, I don't want to talk about anything else. I just want to think about my son."

"This is about Reed."

She paled, reading him like a book. "What have you done?"

"Stay calm."

"I know you and if you want to talk, it's something bad."

He started to keep his secret, but he couldn't. His punishment was so severe that the truth was the only thing that would save him. From himself.

"Remember the dinner party where Reed and Daphne met?"

"Of course. It was a traumatic evening trying to arrange the proper seating."

"I knew Daphne was in town. Clyde and I arranged the meeting."

"What!" Her eyes darkened.

"I had to do something. I could see how Reed felt about Cari."

"So…you thought you'd find Reed a wife who was more suitable."

"Yes." He met the accusation in her eyes squarely.

She shook her head. "Richard… Richard… you promised Marisa and Reed you would not interfere in their lives anymore."

"I know and now I'm being punished." He swallowed hard. "It's my fault Reed is dead."

She stood and put an arm around him. "Oh, Richard. You just never learn, but you're getting a second chance. No." She arched an eyebrow. "This will be your third or fourth."

This calm, understanding reaction wasn't like Vanessa and it threw him. "What are you talking about?"

"Reed's coming home. I mean, I just made cookies and that's something I just don't do."

"It's well known you don't cook. Period."

Now he understood. The woman was out of her mind.

"So you see I'm right. Reed is coming home."

"Or you're losing it."

"It wouldn't be the first time." She kissed his cheek. "Now, let's go to bed and try to sleep. By the way, where is Daphne?"

"I don't know. I would have thought she'd have been back by now."

"Your perfect, suitable wife seems to be an emotional air bag. Or is that vacuum?"

He glared at her for pointing that out.

"Darling, you chose someone just like me. Can't you see that?"

"I'm not in the mood for a lecture."

"Lecture? I thought it was a compliment. I never knew you thought I was the perfect wife."

He didn't know anything anymore. But he had something that could shut off his mind like a tap. He headed for his study.

And the bourbon.

Cari and Reed walked on toward the endless horizon. Cari ached down to her bones, and her feet she couldn't even feel at times, except for the pain. She knew she must have blisters the sizes of quarters on her heels, but she had to keep going. They needed water badly. She was so thirsty, but she tried not to think about it. The sun and the wind were unbearable. She had a tremendous headache and her skin was sunburned and felt like sandpaper.

Something that looked like a tarantula inched across the ground in front of her and she didn't even blink. He was the least of her worries. Her breath was shallow, her lips chafed and dry. All she had to do was pick up her feet and move forward. Her feet were so heavy though. One more step…

She fell to the ground, prostrate, wondering if death was like this, where you reach a point and just give up.

"Cari." She heard Reed's gentle, worried voice.

"Go on without me," she managed to whisper.

"No way," he said. "We go together or we sit right here."

"Reed, you…you…have to find help."

Reed's heart broke as he saw how exhausted she was. He fished out the last of the water. "Drink the water. It'll revive you."

She didn't move.

"Come on, Cari, I never figured you for a quitter."

She didn't respond and he knew she'd reached her limit. Overhead he saw buzzards flying. His chest tightened. *No way.* No way was he going to let her die.

He set the bottle on the ground and gently turned her. Holding her in his arms, he put the bottle to her dry lips. "Drink," he ordered.

She gulped the water and he let her take a breath before he made her drink more. As he held her he saw a prickly pear cactus and then he saw something else. He'd been seeing this cactus for a while and from his school years in Arizona he knew it was cane cholla. It was a thorny tubular segmented bush and the tubular canelike stems drooped toward the ground. The cactus was covered in sharp spines, but clustered among them he saw the yellow egg-shaped fruit. The other bushes he'd noticed didn't have the fruit, so the animals must have eaten them. This was a godsend. It was spiny, too, but he could get to the fruit.

He laid Cari gently on the ground and tucked his jacket beneath her head. She didn't move. He made his way to the cactus and careful of the spines plucked several fruit pods. Splitting one open with his fingers, he carried the fleshy insides to Cari.

"Cari, look. I found more cactus."

She moaned and he helped her to sit up. "Here." He held it to her mouth and she took it and began to eat. He sagged with relief and went back for more.

Thirty minutes later Cari was noticeably better. So was he.

"We'll stay here for the night," he said. "And eat more cactus in the morning before we press on."

"What's the use?" Cari looked at the bleak scenery around her. "We've reached the end of the earth." Suddenly her fighting spirit returned. "Why isn't someone looking for us, damn it? It's like the whole world has forgotten we ever existed."

He tucked her matted hair behind her ear. "Feeling better?"

"A little."

"We're seeing more animals again, so we're getting close to something."

"I saw something that looked weird, but I was too tired to pay it much attention."

"It was a ringtail. I saw it, too. It looks like a cross between a raccoon and a cat."

"That was it." She sighed. "I don't even care anymore."

Reed glanced toward the sinking sun. "We might as well try and get some rest."

Cari winced.

"What?"

"My feet hurt so badly."

"Lie back on my jacket and I'll look at your feet."

"It's just blisters."

"Lie back, please."

"You can be really annoying sometimes." But she stretched out and put her feet in his lap.

Her sneakers were a filthy dirt-brown color, as were her socks. Slipping off the shoes, he saw the socks were stuck to the sides of her heels. Definitely blisters.

"Sit tight. I'm going to get more cactus." Within minutes he had what he wanted. Sitting cross-legged, he lifted her feet. "I'm going to remove your socks. Take a deep breath."

"Oh, ouch!" She made a face.

As he looked closely at the raw irritated spots, he saw they had rubbed through her hose. He wondered how she was walking at all.

"Are these knee-highs?"

"Yes."

"I'm going to remove them." Slowly he peeled off the dirty hosiery and gently rubbed the soft, jelly-like cactus all over the sores. Then he did the same to her sunburned face and his. "Let's leave your socks off until morning and give the sores some air."

"Okay."

He gathered her close, letting her use his body as a cushion. Luckily there was grass here, so the ground wasn't so hard. He shook out his jacket with one hand and pulled it over them.

The night desert sounds surrounded them. Coyotes howled, crickets chirped, the wind rustled, yet there was a quiet that was unnerving and unending.

She snuggled closer. "My feet feel better. Thank you."

"You're welcome."

"Look at those stars," she said. "Aren't they beautiful?"

"Like beacons guiding us home."

"Home," she murmured. "That sounds so nice, but I wonder if we're even going in the right direction."

"Like we decided from the start, if we keep

going east, using the sun as our guide, we should come upon something."

"Or we could be completely lost."

He squeezed her playfully. "Is this the same girl who thumbed her nose at 'Mr. Jerk'?"

"Mr. Cool," she corrected.

"Mr. Jerk," he stated emphatically.

She giggled, a lighthearted sound that warmed his heart. "Okay, Mr. Jerk." She was still for a moment. "Your logic about our direction sounds reasonable, but it's so frustrating."

"We'll make it. We just have to regain our strength."

Her hand touched his beard. "So woolly."

"Mmm."

"And sexy."

He looked down at her. "You think so?"

"Definitely. If I wasn't so tired I might..."

He cuddled her closer.

He might, too.

Chapter Ten

Cari woke up with sand in her mouth. Sitting up, she wiped her mouth on her sleeve and encountered more dirt. Damn! She wasn't so tired though and that was a good thing. Her feet felt much better, too.

She raised a foot to inspect her heel and heard a sound. Glancing up, she saw two wolves or coyotes with shaggy coats growling at them, teeth bared. Hair stood up on their backs. Goose bumps rippled across her skin.

"Easy," Reed whispered beside her.

Cari had had enough. She wasn't afraid. Picking up a rock, she threw it as hard as she could and screamed, "Get the hell away. We are not your breakfast."

The rock hit one of the animals. He yelped and sprinted away, the other one following.

"Well, that did the trick," Reed said, gently rubbing her neck. "Fearless Cari."

She leaned her head on his arm. "I've never been more afraid. Not of those stupid animals." She sucked in a breath. "I'm afraid of dying. Are you?"

He gazed into her eyes. "Cari…"

"I'm not afraid of the actual dying part or finding out about the hereafter. I'm afraid of the things I've left undone or unsaid."

"Like what?"

She watched the beautiful sunrise and its dazzling colors as it bathed the bleakness of the west Texas landscape with a vitality that was unique and awesome.

"Remember when I talked about what I'd do if I had all the time in the world?"

"Sure."

"Well, it wouldn't be soaking in a spa with champagne and strawberries. I'd call my mom and talk for hours. No, better yet, I'd go home and spend the day with her in her kitchen and just soak up the smell of her cooking and her loving heart. My mom is a great cook and she loves it when her girls are in the kitchen with her."

"My mother doesn't know how to boil water."

She looked at him. "Does Daphne?"

He frowned. "I have no idea. It wasn't what I loved about her."

She wondered if he realized he'd used past tense. Any other time, any other place, she would have pointed that out and asked what it was he did love about Daphne. She realized though he had to come to terms with his own feelings about his fiancée. And Cari had to respect those feelings. She wasn't beating herself up about it anymore. She just wanted to live.

"What else would you do?"

"Take my sisters and my nieces shopping. They're always bugging me to, but I never have time. And I would ride in the cab of the tractor with my dad and sing along to the country music he has playing on the radio. Then I'd just listen to him talk about the olden days and how tough times were. Afterward I would apologize for ever being embarrassed to wear hand-me-down clothes, because he'd given me the greatest gift of all—unconditional love."

For a moment there was silence as she realized what a wonderful childhood she'd really had. She also realized her job wasn't her life. She had so much more.

She stood and stretched. "What would you do if you had all the time in the world?"

He shrugged as he rose to his feet. "I've always had all the time in the world except when I became CEO of Dalton's. Fitting everything into my life became a challenge, but time has always been my own."

"Mmm. The old silver spoon in your mouth, huh?"

"You could say that." He headed for the cactus. "How about breakfast?"

"Since coffee is out, cactus sounds yummy."

Reed plucked several more egg-shaped fruit. They sat and ate until they didn't want any more, and then Reed rubbed more cacti over her blisters.

He leaned back on his heels, a thoughtful expression on his face. "I'm thinking about that all-the-time-in-the-world thing."

"And?"

"I think I would like to sit in your mom's kitchen and watch her cook and I'd enjoy riding on the tractor with your dad."

She grinned. "You've been out in the sun too long."

"No. I've just never had that type of life filled with love and caring."

She didn't bring up Daphne. It would serve no purpose. "Well, Junior, when we make it home, I'll introduce you to a simple way of life."

"You're on."

She made a face at her dirty socks, but pulled them on anyway and gently shoved her feet into the sneakers, trying not to wince. The damaged hose she stuffed into the backpack.

Reed wiped dust from his boots. "I haven't had these off in days and my feet feel fine."

"Yeah." Cari stood. "Colter's company makes you custom boots and what do I get? Wait until I see him."

"I don't think cowboy boots would go with your power suits."

"Maybe I'll start a new trend."

She wasn't sure about the future or of what lay ahead for her. Her whole way of thinking had changed. She watched as Reed slipped on the backpack. Her feelings for him would never change and she would no longer hide them. Or deny them. Or flaunt them. She would graciously accept that he didn't love her. But he had to say it to her face.

One day.

Soon.

"Time to go," Reed said, putting as much of the fruit as he could in the backpack.

She fell into step beside him. They walked in silence and Cari tried to ignore the pain in her feet. They were now in a valley of tall weeds and grasses. Several deer loped in front of them and they stopped to watch the graceful creatures until they disappeared into the vast landscape.

As they continued, Cari's legs grew tired again and that lethargic feeling settled over her. She didn't know how much longer she could keep going.

The wind tugged at her with brutal strength, but she didn't give in. After she stumbled a couple of times, Reed finally stopped and they rested in the shade of a shrubby oak and listened to the howling of the wind. They ate more cactus.

"Would you like to take off your sneakers?" Reed asked, finishing a fruit pod.

"No."

"Are you okay?"

She nodded. But she wasn't sure. She was

just bone tired and dirty. A sense of helplessness invaded her well of strength and she laid her head on his shoulder.

"I'm supposed to be the weaker sex and I guess I'm proving it."

"Cari Michaels weak? That just doesn't compute."

"You could make better time if you went alone."

"Look around you," he said instead of answering.

She raised her head. "What?" She saw the same old scenery.

"The grass is getting taller and greener and there are more trees. We're seeing lots of animals. That can only mean one thing."

"Water," she murmured as she watched a couple of antelope run by with amazing speed.

"Yes. We're definitely getting close to something."

Cari pushed to her feet. "Let's go then."

He pulled her back down. "We have to rest."

"Oh, I love a strong man."

"Even one who looks like the hairy man?"

"You bet." She rested her head on his shoulder again and closed her eyes. In her mind's eye they were dressed to the nines as they sailed across a ballroom dance floor to a slow Texas waltz.

He loved her.

She loved him.

And delirium never seemed so right.

Richard awoke to a throbbing head. He lay on the sofa in his study fully dressed in yesterday's clothes. An empty bottle of bourbon stood on the coffee table.

He sat up and held his head with both hands. Getting drunk had solved nothing nor helped to ease his discontent. He was afraid nothing would.

His son was gone.

Today that was still true.

The door opened and Vanessa walked in dressed in brown slacks and a peach silk blouse.

She glared at his disheveled appearance. "Richard, for heaven's sake, pull yourself together."

"Go away, Vanessa." A composed Vanessa at this time of the morning was irritating.

"I will not. Reporters are at the gate wanting a statement, and TV stations are calling for an interview. If you're not up to it, I'll

write a statement for your secretary to give
to the press."

He squinted at her, wondering if this was
really his wife, the one who was consumed
with her life and only her life. When did she
get so damn strong? Why in the hell wasn't
she grieving like him?

He rose to his feet gingerly and the room
spun. He reached for the arm of the sofa, but
Vanessa was there to give him a hand. For the
first time in his life he leaned on her.

"Go upstairs and take a shower. I'll deal
with the press."

"I'll be okay in a minute," he said, trying to
maintain his balance. "I'll handle the media."

She looked at him. "Are you worried I can't
do it?"

"I'm worried about what you'll say."

"Richard, just because I refuse to say my
son is dead doesn't make me crazy. I... I
know Reed may never come back, but please
let me have that dream no matter how erro-
neous it may be. I need to believe my son is
still alive. For now, I need that."

His arms went around her and he held her
tight, something he hadn't done in a very long
time. "Okay. I'll go shower and we'll write
a statement together. Call Nancy and let her

know we'll have something soon for her to dispense, and tell Winston to call the police to get rid of the people at the gate."

"Will do," she replied, and they stared at each other for endless moments. "We'll get through this," she added. "Our daughter and her family are having breakfast and we need to join them."

"Give me ten minutes." He started for the door and turned abruptly. He walked to her and kissed her cheek. As he moved away, he saw she held her hand to the spot he'd touched.

Maybe there was hope for redemption after all.

Cari and Reed kept walking. He adjusted his stride to hers, but in truth he was growing weary. He had to stay strong for her. They didn't talk. It took too much energy.

The wind had died down and that helped. They ate the last of the cacti, but they needed water. Badly.

They saw it at the same time and came to a complete stop. A narrow silver ribbon haphazardly threaded its way through the landscape. A creek! Water!

"Oh my God," Cari said and took off running. Somehow the sight had given her a burst of energy. She fell halfway there and Reed picked her up and with their arms wrapped around each other they quickly made their way to the water's edge.

Cari lay flat on her stomach in the weeds and scooped water into her hands and drank. "Heavenly," she gushed. "And it even looks clean."

He joined her and did likewise. "Drink slowly," he instructed.

After a few minutes they sat up, taking deep breaths. "We made it," he said. "Life can't be far away."

She glanced at the water. "This creek is probably dry most of the time, but because of the thunderstorm that caused the crash it has water. Thank God."

"If we keep following it, we're bound to come to a small town or even a ranch. Soon we'll be rescued."

"I'm hoping very soon." Cari continued to stare at the water. "What do you think is below the surface, snakes, frogs, turtles and other amphibious creatures?"

"I'm sure there is, and ordinarily the water probably wouldn't be safe to drink."

"We have no choice though." She began to unbutton her blouse. "I'm going swimming."

"I don't think that's a good idea. You're very weak and..." His voice trailed away as she pulled her blouse free and threw it on the ground. Her upper arms were blue, almost purple, and her hands, neck and face were scorched red with sunburn.

She placed her hands on her hips. "Well, Junior, if you don't want to see a dirty naked woman, you'd better close your eyes."

Next she removed her sneakers and peeled away her socks, wincing. Then she unzipped her slacks and removed them. Once again he noticed black-and-blue spots on her legs and back. It had to be from the crash, yet she had nursed him without one word of complaint about her own pain.

When she undid her bra and removed her panties, he should have looked away, but he didn't. He couldn't. He had to see everything that was Cari. The lines of her body were slim yet rounded in all the right places. Her breasts were full and her hips swayed suggestively as she strolled toward the water. As he watched her naked backside, something came alive in him.

Desire.

As exhausted as he was, he still felt it. He remembered all the times he'd experienced the same thing working side by side with her. And denied it just as many.

She could make him angrier than anyone. She could frustrate him to the very end of his patience, and she could lift him up in ways he'd never acknowledged before. She made him want to be a better person. A better man.

What about Daphne?

He had a hard time remembering his fiancée's face.

He pushed the thought away as Cari stepped into the water. It might be deep and she was exhausted. He was instantly on his feet.

"Cari," he shouted, but she waded in and floated around.

"It's wonderful." She smiled and his breath lodged in his throat. She was so beautiful. "Join me."

He shook his head and watched as she splashed around, going under several times and shaking the water from her sunburned face.

"Chicken," she called.

He stood there feeling all the restrictions that had been placed on him by birth. *He wasn't an ordinary child and had to maintain neatness, order and control.* Reed Preston wasn't an ordinary man. But out here, he was just like everyone else.

An ordinary man lived life to the fullest.

Sitting down in the grass, he removed his boots and socks and wiggled his toes in the warm air for the first time in days. Then he stripped away his shirt, jeans and briefs. He saw the bruises on his body, too, but didn't give them a second thought.

He jumped into the water and came up a few feet from her. The water was heavenly just as she'd said. One look into her dark eyes and he glimpsed paradise.

He swam toward her and gathered her into his arms. Her wet naked body moved temptingly against his and any self-control he had vanished.

"What do you think?" she asked.

"I think you had the right idea."

She grinned and wrapped her legs around his waist in a provocative movement. "All we need is soap."

"Mmm." He kissed the warm hollow of her neck. "I think we have all we need."

She wiggled and he tried to keep them both afloat. As they played around, their laughter carried on the wind. When his feet touched bottom, he swung her up into his arms and carried her to the green grass.

He gently laid her down and was mesmerized by the passion in her dark eyes. He wanted her. It was that plain. That simple.

Yet complicated.

He was engaged to someone else and he didn't take that lightly.

"Cari, I'm sorry." He lay beside her and knew he wasn't an ordinary man.

He was a saint.

Chapter Eleven

Cari stared up at the bright blue sky not feeling hurt at his words. She knew him well enough to know he was struggling with the dictates of his life and his choices. She wondered though if that even mattered out here.

"Do you believe in destiny or fate?" she asked.

"Sure."

She leaned up on one elbow to look at him. They lay side by side without a stitch of clothes and yet it felt so right. The lean lines of his body were marred only by bruises, and the beard gave him a sinister yet sexy look. So many times she'd dreamed of a situation like this—with just the two of them. This might be her only chance, her last chance, and she wasn't letting it slip away.

"I believe we were meant to be here together."

His eyes darkened but he didn't say anything.

She touched his chest, tentatively at first, and then splayed her hand across his breastbone, feeling his heart beating rapidly against her palm.

"Out here you're not my boss. We're just a man and a woman. Alone. The rest of the world doesn't exist." She trailed one finger through the hair narrowing down to his stomach. His skin felt rough, exciting and warm.

She was tempting him and any other time, any other place, she would know this was wrong. They may not have a tomorrow so she was taking today.

The right or wrong would come later.

She replaced her finger with her lips and he groaned, cupping her head and pulling her up to him.

"Oh, Cari." His voice was a throaty whisper, his eyes as dark as she'd ever seen them.

She kissed his lips gently, the touch of his beard arousing. "This is here. This is now. I don't know if it's right or if it's wrong. I just know that I love you and I want you to make love to me." She kissed him again, feeling a response yet a hesitation. "Other than that I do not expect one thing from you."

His hands still cupped her face and he took her lips fully and with passion. He pulled her on top of him, their bodies welding together, her breasts pressed into the hairs on his chest, soft on hard, breast to breast, hips on hips. She'd never felt anything more erotic.

"You're so beautiful, so tempting," he breathed between her lips, his hands trailing down the curve of her naked back. "I want you more than anything I've ever wanted in my life."

"I'm yours," she murmured and he deepened the kiss to a level they both needed. His tongue tasted and explored and the blood surged through her veins as she returned his passion with a fervor of her own. Whatever tiredness she'd felt vanished at his first caress.

No mouthwash, no soap, no cologne or perfume, yet the touch of his hands and lips on her body was so primal and arousing that she couldn't get enough. His hardness pressed into her and she luxuriated in his maleness, his power.

He rolled her over and his lips found her nipple, sucking, teasing, unleashing an urgency in her that she'd never felt before. The brush of his beard seemed to heighten her senses. His hands stroked, teased until she was on fire with wanting him.

She needed to touch and feel as well, and her hands found his male prowess, feeling every masculine inch of him. He moaned but didn't stop her.

When Cari reached the point of no return, she opened her legs and Reed thrust into her. Their dismal world faded away and they were two people needing each other. His lips took hers in a fierce need and her hands splayed across his back as each thrust took them closer and closer to the precipice of unadulterated pleasure.

As shudders of release pulsatcd though her body, she cried, "Reed. Oh, Reed, I love you."

He trembled his release and buried his face in the warmth of her neck. "Cari," he breathed hoarsely.

Exhausted in a new way, she stroked his hair and stared up at pure blue sky, knowing she would never feel anything like this again—this joining of two souls.

* * *

Reed held on to every nuance of emotion that transformed his body from tired and weary into strong and powerful. Cari did that by just being Cari. He could no longer deny what he felt for her was real. He couldn't acknowledge it either. She understood he had commitments, responsibilities. For now they had each other and they both needed that. He rolled away, taking Cari with him and holding her close against his side, feeling at peace for the first time in days.

As he looked around, there was something gentler about the scenery. It wasn't as desolate as the land they had covered. Here was water and hope. Soon they would find civilization and return to Dallas, but that seemed like another world. Another man had lived that life. Right now all he could think about was the woman in his arms.

He glanced down at her and she was sound asleep, her features serene, her dark eyes closed, her short hair plastered against her head. She'd never looked more beautiful. He kissed her forehead and followed her into a peaceful slumber.

The warm sun on his skin woke him and he scrambled up, as did Cari. The last thing they needed was more sunburn, especially on their naked bodies. They stared at each other for endless seconds.

She placed a finger over his lips. "No regrets?"

"No regrets," he whispered and kissed her deeply. Finally he asked, "Ready to start walking? I feel if we follow the creek it will lead somewhere, a town maybe or a ranch."

She made a face. "I'd rather stay right here and live in the moment."

He kissed the blue marks on her arm. "Cari, we need to talk."

She picked up her bra and panties. Her skin was smooth, soft, perfect, and he wanted to pull her back into his arms.

She hooked her bra. "Why do we need to talk?"

"Aren't you angry I didn't say I love you back?"

She stuck her feet into her panties and pulled them up. "No, because I know you can't say it until you're free. I told you I didn't expect one thing from you."

He found his briefs and slipped into them. "You're lying. We crossed the line here today, but it was a line I was willing to cross. For you I think I'd do just about anything."

"I know." She smiled slightly. "Now let's find our way to civilization and home so we can sort out our future."

When he bent to pick up his jeans, she said, "Do you know you have a very sexy butt? Buns of steel."

He grinned. "I don't believe anyone has ever told me that."

"Take my word for it. You do."

"I could say the same about yours. Your breasts aren't bad either."

She giggled and buttoned her blouse. "Why, thank you, kind sir."

Sitting down, he pulled on his boots. "We're a matching black-and-blue pair."

"Hopefully those will heal."

He stood and kissed her briefly. "Ready?"

She smiled into his eyes. "Yes."

Within a few minutes they were fully dressed. Reed filled the water bottles and they were off again to face that future.

Their future.

Whatever it might be.

Two hours later they were exhausted once again. The creek ended abruptly, so they knew it wasn't a flowing creek, just a gully filled with rainwater. The signs of human life they'd hoped for weren't there. Cari tried to stay strong, but her feet hurt so badly she could barely stand. Her head throbbed and her skin felt on fire from sunburn. Reed wrapped his arms around her waist and carried her at times.

The wind picked up again and blew against them until Cari's strength was gone. She couldn't go on. Sinking to the ground, she gave in to the pain and the disillusionment.

"I can't…go any farther."

Reed sat beside her and placed his jacket over their heads as the wind howled around them. He fished the water out of the backpack.

"Drink," he said.

The water tasted great even though she saw some sediment in it. She drank it anyway.

Reed took a swallow. "We'll rest for a bit."

"No one knows we're alive, so no one is looking for us."

"Shh." He pulled her close. "Just rest."

She pulled away. "What good is rest? We're going to die," she shouted.

"No, we're not," he shouted back.

"I can't keep going," she said in despair.

"Then I'll carry you."

"No. You have to go on without me."

"We've had this conversation, Cari, and the answer is still the same. No."

"God. You're stubborn."

"Just stop arguing. You're using unnecessary strength. Save it for walking."

"Yes, Junior." She laid her head on his shoulder, knowing why she loved this man. He had more character than anyone she'd ever met and it went all the way to his soul.

When the wind died down, they stood and trudged on. Reed kept his arm around her waist and her feet barely touched the ground.

How long could they continue to do this?

By noon Richard's headache was gone. The family ate a light lunch and adjourned to the living room.

"We really need to think about making arrangements," he said.

"No," Vanessa replied sharply. "It's too soon. Wait until the investigation is finished."

"That could take weeks."

She lifted an eyebrow. "So?"

He took a deep breath. "We can't continue to live like this. We need to put Reed to rest."

"Richard, I absolutely refuse."

"Listen, Vanessa. I spoke to Fletcher's ex-wife and Melody's parents and they're already planning memorial services. I feel we need to do the same."

Vanessa shook her head. "Absolutely not."

Marisa put an arm around her mother. "I agree. Let's wait. We all need time."

"Sweetheart…" The doorbell rang, stopping him.

"Oh." Vanessa hurried toward the door. "That's Ruth and Sam. I invited them and told Winston to let them in."

Richard frowned. "They're back!"

Marisa linked her arm through his. "This is what Mother needs, so please be patient. And courteous."

"I'll try." He nodded. "Where's Colter?"

"He's in the backyard with the kids. They're not used to being cooped up in a house all the time and they need a break from the sadness."

"So do you," he told her.

"I'm trying to be strong." Her voice wobbled.

"Marisa."

"I'll be okay," she said. "As long as I have Colter and the kids, I can be strong."

As he looked at his daughter, his past manipulations weighed heavily upon him and he now knew the full price of controlling his children's lives. The price was a pain so great he didn't know if he'd ever survive.

The Michaelses and their four children walked into the room. Were these people ever going to leave him alone?

"Look, Richard." Vanessa held up a bag. "Ruth brought me yarn and needles. Wasn't that kind?"

In response, he turned and started for his study.

Marisa caught his arm and pulled him down by her on the sofa. Now he was stuck, but no way would he disappoint his daughter.

He'd done enough of that.

By late afternoon, Reed was literally dragging Cari and he had to stop. Despair settled over him and he noticed the buzzards circling overhead. This was it. Neither of them had the strength to go on.

They had no more water. He held Cari, knowing he would hold her until his last breath. His throat was dry, his skin was burned by the sun and he ached in every bone and muscle of his body.

Cacti were all around them, and as soon as he had more strength he'd scrounge for more cactus fruit.

"Cari." He shook her.

"Hmm." She moved her head against him, but she was out.

Glancing to the distant horizon, he prayed as he'd never prayed before. He blinked as he saw something and wondered if it was his imagination. It seemed like a dust cloud. Placing his jacket under Cari's head, he carefully rose to his feet. She lay prone, not moving.

The cloud of dust moved closer and it wasn't his imagination. It was something!

He bent down. "I'll be right back," he told Cari.

She didn't respond.

Slipping off the backpack, he started toward the dust. He didn't want to get too far away from Cari or lose his way. Through the weeds he walked as fast as he was able and then he saw it—a dirt track that was probably a road.

Thank God!

An old truck came into view and Reed ran forward, waving his arms. The vehicle came to a stop and dust suffocated him. He coughed and ran to the passenger door.

Luckily the window was down and a Mexican man somewhere in his sixties peered back at him.

"What you doing out here, mister?" the man asked. He spoke English.

"Our plane crashed." He took a breath. "Do you have a phone?"

"Sí. But it no work good out here."

"Please try to call the authorities and tell them there are survivors from the Dalton plane crash."

He frowned and looked around. "Survivors?"

"Yes, but she's in bad shape. We need help badly. I'll go and get her."

"I'll help."

"No. Call."

"Sí."

Richard sat between Marisa and Kitty and thought he couldn't listen to one more word of this family togetherness.

Vanessa sat by Ruth, patiently listening to her instructions on knitting.

The others were quiet, as if in a holding pattern.

Kitty patted his arm. "Relax, Mr. Preston."

He gave her a hard look. "Under the circumstances that's impossible."

She flicked back her hair. "I know what you mean."

Loud voices at the door distracted them. Everyone got to their feet.

Mr. Avery rushed in white as a sheet.

Richard hurried to him. "What is it?"

He took a long breath. "Two survivors have been found from the crash."

Loud voices in the door interrupted him.
Footsteps came to their feet.
Mr. Avery rolled by the bed.
Richard hurried to meet them at the
It took a long time before
heard right from the crash

Chapter Twelve

No one moved or said a word.

"What?" Richard's voice was barely audible.

Mr. Avery took another long breath. "I'm sorry. I'm out of breath. I ran all the way to my car when I heard the news. I wanted to tell you in person." He drew in deeply. "We got a call from the sheriff in Jeff Davis County. We've been in touch with all law enforcement in surrounding counties. He said a man found two survivors of the Dalton plane crash."

"Two survivors?" Richard asked, his palms sweaty.

"Yes. That's all I know. A medevac helicopter from Midland is on the way. It was the closest. They can get to them faster than anyone."

Richard swallowed. "Who are the survivors?"

"We don't know. The static on the man's phone who called it in prevented the sheriff from getting details. The man said there were two survivors and one was in bad shape."

"Four people were on that plane," Richard said almost to himself. *His son could be one of the survivors.*

He looked Avery straight in the eye. "I want names and I want them now."

"I'm sorry, Mr. Preston, you'll have to wait like everyone else. The helicopter pilot has instructions to call as soon as he locates them."

"Listen, goddammit…"

"Richard." He turned to Vanessa and she motioned for him to join them. She reached for Ruth's hand. "Ruth, would you pray, please?"

They all linked hands. Without a second thought he walked to his wife and took her hand, and then his daughter's. They bowed their heads and Ruth said a prayer. When it was finished, Richard kept praying.

If you let one of the survivors be my son, I

promise to never interfere in his life again. I will confess all my shady dealings and change my ways. Just let him live. Let him have a life of his choosing.

Now they waited. No one sat down. They were too nervous. Soon they'd know if their children were dead or alive.

This tiny sliver of hope was almost worse than before.

This time the news would be final.

Darin Avery took command of Richard's study, checking the progress of the helicopter. Richard held on to Vanessa's hand. For some reason he needed to. He was so afraid he was now going to be punished beyond anything he'd ever imagined. And he would need Vanessa in those moments.

Reed carried Cari to the truck. She was so sunburned, so still.

The Mexican ran to help him.

"It's okay," he said. "Please open the door."

The man obliged, his eyes on Cari's limp body. "Is she dead?"

"No," Reed replied, sliding onto the seat.

The man hurried around to the driver's side.

"Did you reach the authorities?"

"Sí. I called the sheriff and he said he'd send help. I told him we'd be on this old dirt road and gave him the location."

"Thank you. Do you have any water?"

"Sure. Never go without water out here." He reached on the floorboard and handed Reed a water jug.

Reed managed to pour some into the lid and held it to Cari's dry lips. "It's water, Cari. Taste it."

She moaned and he dampened her lips.

"Drink, Cari, please. We're going home."

She licked her lips and he tipped the lid and she swallowed. "That's it. Keep drinking."

"Re-ed."

"Shh. We're going home."

Her head fell against his chest and he let her sleep. Soon she'd have medical attention.

The man slowly began to drive. "My name is Pedro," he said.

"Pedro, you saved our lives." Reed took several swallows from the jug.

"How long y'all been walking, mister?"

"Days. My name is Reed Preston. Can you get a signal on your phone?"

Pedro picked up the cell from the seat and flipped it open. "It still has a lot of static. It comes and goes."

"Do you live around here?"

"I live not far out of Fort Davis. I check oil pump meters on the oil wells."

"We didn't see any oil wells."

Pedro flung his arm out the window. "Farther that way. I'm just returning from a run."

"So Fort Davis is the closest town?"

"Sí."

The plane had veered severely off course. Reed closed his eyes as he thought of Fletcher and Melody.

The road was bumpy, but Reed didn't mind. It was the best ride of his life. They rode in silence and Reed was glad. He didn't have any strength left.

"Look." Pedro pointed to the sky.

Reed saw the big helicopter and a feeling of relief suffused his body. Now Cari would get help.

"Stop," he said and Pedro slammed on the brakes.

Reed waited until the big bird found a landing spot and then he got out, holding tightly to Cari. "Thank you, Pedro."

"Sí." He nodded. "God go with you."

The doors of the helicopter opened and three men jumped out with a stretcher.

"Cari, we're going home."

* * *

"The medevac is on the ground," Mr. Avery said and everyone gathered around, waiting for the magical words.

The wait stretched.

"What the hell is taking so long?" Richard snapped.

Mr. Avery held up a hand and switched to speakerphone. "Sir, we have a white female in bad shape. She barely has a pulse and is severely sunburned and dehydrated, but she's alive."

"What's her name?" Sam asked as he held his wife's hand.

There was a long pause and mumbled voices could be heard in the background.

"Cari Michaels," came through loud and clear.

"Oh, oh." Ruth began to cry. "Thank God. Thank God!" The family embraced tightly and then they all waited again.

"Who's the other survivor?" Mr. Avery asked.

Richard's voice was lodged in his throat. All he could do was hold on to Vanessa's hand. Marisa wrapped her arm around him and they waited for the name. Colter walked in and joined them.

"Sorry, sir, this is taking a moment," the voice came through. "The second survivor has just collapsed. We're trying to revive him."

"We need a name," Mr. Avery said. "Families are waiting. Just give us a name."

A long moment followed and more muffled voices. Then the voice came again, "The man who found them said the man called himself Reed Preston."

Ohmygod! His prayers had been answered. *His son was alive.*

Richard's knees buckled, but he managed to keep standing. Vanessa sobbed tears of joy and Marisa clung to Colter.

The Michaels family walked over and they all embraced, and Richard clung just like the rest.

"Our children are alive," Ruth said. "We have been blessed."

"Both patients are loaded and we're headed for Midland," came through on the phone.

"No." Richard immediately took charge. "If their injuries are not life threatening, please bring them to Dallas—to the Dallas Medical Center."

"Is that possible?" Mr. Avery asked into the phone.

"Just a minute, sir. The patients are being evaluated."

They waited again.

"All go here. We're headed for Dallas."

"Thank you," Richard replied.

"We have to be there when they arrive," Vanessa said, brushing away tears. They hurried for the door.

Richard hung back. "Thank you, Mr. Avery," he said.

"I'm glad your son and Ms. Michaels are alive. It's as close to a miracle as I've ever seen." He swiped a hand through his hair. "Now I have to meet with the other two families. They've been told there were two survivors."

"I have already spoken to them, but I will be contacting them again to offer my condolences."

"I'm sure they'd appreciate that."

"Please let them know that whatever they need is at their disposal courtesy of the Preston family and Dalton's."

Mr. Avery nodded.

"Richard." Vanessa rushed back into the room. "Let's go see our son."

He linked his arm through hers. Today was a day for miracles and he embraced that knowledge with all his heart. His son was alive.

Now Richard had to tell him the truth.

He'd promised.

Before God.

The waiting at the hospital grew intense. The men paced and the women huddled together. Colter had dropped the kids at his sister's and was soon back, but the medevac still wasn't in sight.

They had strict orders not to walk out to the helicopter pad, so they waited just inside the hospital, the pad in view. Richard just wanted to see his son.

They ran to the large windows as they saw the helicopter hovering above the landing site. It landed smoothly. The door flew open and a stretcher was lowered to the ground. Hospital personnel rushed through the double doors to meet the paramedics. The stretcher was pushed through to the waiting E.R. team.

Cari Michaels was on the stretcher, her hair plastered to her head, her skin sunburned and dirty. Richard hardly recognized her. Sam and Ruth hurried to the stretcher before they could roll her away.

"Cari, baby, it's Mama." Ruth kissed her forehead.

"Hey, sweet girl," Sam said, his voice cracking.

Cari didn't respond and Ruth dissolved into tears while Judith and Kitty hugged her. Her brothers stood stoically by their father.

Richard turned as the other stretcher was rolled in and for a moment he forgot to breathe. Vanessa and Marisa ran to Reed's side, but Richard's feet seemed glued to the floor. The man on the bed didn't look like his son. He had a growth of beard, a gash on his head and he was sunburned and filthy from head to toe.

Vanessa stroked Reed's face. "Darling, it's Mother."

Marisa kissed him a moment before they wheeled him away.

"The doctor will be out after he's checked them over," a nurse said. "Try to relax. There's a cafeteria downstairs."

"Thank you," Marisa said. "We'll wait right here."

The families adjourned to the waiting room, but Richard was rooted to the spot. He'd seen his son and he was alive. But was Reed okay?

What had the crash done to him mentally? Was this nightmare ever going to end?

Richard heard the *tip-tap* of high heels before he saw Daphne.

"Richard." She walked up to him. "I heard they found survivors from the crash. Is that true?"

"Yes, Daphne, it's true."

Her eyes narrowed. "Why wasn't I notified?"

"I'm sorry. It's been a very trying time."

"Winston said one of the survivors is Reed. I really resent not being notified."

Richard saw the fire in her blue eyes, but it didn't faze him. "To tell you the truth I didn't have a clue where you were, off giving interviews or whatever you deemed so important. My only focus is my son, and everything and everyone else can just go to hell."

"I do not appreciate that tone, but I understand you're upset." She took a breath. "Where is Reed? Is he okay?"

Richard was wondering when she'd get around to Reed. "He's in the E.R. They're working on him."

"I can't believe it. I'm so happy. I want to see him as soon as possible."

Before Richard could answer, Daphne

looked at the people in the waiting room. "Who are those people?"

"Cari Michaels's family."

"She's one of the survivors?"

"Yes."

As Daphne contemplated this, a swarm of reporters descended on them, firing questions. Richard was drained and at the end of his rope. Sammy and Chase marched them right out the door. They both were over six feet and heavily muscled, while the reporters were smaller of stature and soft. No way were they going to put up a fuss.

The doctor came out and their attention was on him. He introduced himself as Dr. Benton. "Ms. Michaels is severely dehydrated," he said. "She's sunburned and has blisters on her feet. Her body is bruised, but she doesn't have any major injuries. Mr. Preston is basically the same, sunburned, bruised and dehydrated. He has a gash over his left temple that has started to heal. They haven't had food in several days so they are understandably weak. We'll start the refeeding process slowly. They are both still out, but they're getting intravenous fluid, so I feel they'll come out of it soon. Right now they need to rest and heal. Thankfully they are going to be fine."

"Thank you." Daphne hugged the doctor.

Dr. Benton seemed disconcerted. "And you are?"

"Daphne Harwood. Reed Preston's fiancée."

"Oh."

"I'd like to see him as soon as possible."

"Mr. Preston is not conscious. He won't know if you're there or not."

"But I will." Her mouth formed a pout. "Please."

The doctor wasn't moved. "They will be moved to the Intensive Care Unit. I want them monitored for twenty-four hours. You can see him at the scheduled visiting hours."

"Oh, thank you."

"How long will it be before my daughter is in ICU?" Sam asked.

"In about an hour. But check with the nurse for visiting hours."

"I will. Thank you."

Dr. Benton nodded. "This will be something they'll be able to tell their grandchildren. They are both very lucky to have made it out alive."

"We're very grateful," Ruth said. "We'll go to the ICU and wait."

The Michaels family trailed toward the elevators and the doc turned to go back to the E.R. Richard caught his arm. "I'm Richard Preston, Reed's father, and I really need to see my son."

"Like I said…"

"Don't give me that bull. I demand to see my son now and you might want to check with the CEO of this hospital to find out how much money I've donated for various fund-raisers. I'm not trying to throw my weight around, but up until a couple of hours ago I thought my son was dead. Five minutes is all I'm asking."

The doctor bristled as Richard knew he would. "We're very busy saving lives in the E.R. and we'd rather not have families inter-fering with our work."

Richard glared at him as he had so many times in his past when he was determined to get his way.

Dr. Benton swallowed. "Five minutes."

"Thank you."

"Richard, do you have to be so pigheaded?" Vanessa asked. "Our son is alive. Let him have some peace. We'll see him in the ICU. The Michaels family understands that. Why can't you?"

He ran a hand through his hair. "Vanessa."

She walked closer to him. Marisa, Colter and Daphne stood some distance away. "Don't you say one word to Reed that will upset him in any way."

"I would never do that."

"Oh, please." Vanessa rolled her eyes. "This is about you and your desire for forgiveness. Once again we stand the risk of losing our child because of your insatiable desire for control. Let's don't do it today. Let's just celebrate his life and sort out the dirty laundry later." She touched his arm. "Apologize to Dr. Benton and let's go up to the ICU. We'll see our son when we're supposed to."

"Vanessa, I…"

"No, you don't. Apologize."

Richard knew she was right and he had a feeling he wasn't going to like this calm, rational woman. The self-centered one suited his life. She never interfered with his decisions. But their whole lives had changed in a matter of a few days and he had to acquiesce as she wanted him to.

That's how he started to make up for all the wrong he'd done.

He shoved his hands into his slacks pockets. "Dr. Benton, I'm sorry. I'm just worried about my son. I'll see him in the ICU."

Dr. Benton inclined his head. "I'll let the head nurse know you can see your son as soon as they have him comfortable."

"I'd appreciate that."

Vanessa linked her arm through his. "I'm very proud of you, dear. Let's go join the Michaelses."

Proud of him? She'd never said that before. Stepping back. Letting go. He'd never done that before either. He had a feeling a lot more changes were yet to come.

Chapter Thirteen

Reed's head throbbed, but he wouldn't give in to it. He had to stay focused and get Cari to the truck. They were going home.

Something was wrong. Different. His body felt relaxed and he wasn't lying on the ground. Where was he? Where was Cari?

With extreme effort he opened his eyes and a soft light seemed to surround him. He was in a room—a hospital room and an IV dripped into his arm. They'd been rescued!

Where was Cari? Through a large window he could see a nurses' station directly ahead. Other than that he couldn't see anything else. He was so tired, but he had to find out about Cari.

A nurse walked in and adjusted the IV. "Oh, Mr. Preston, you're awake."

"Where's Cari Michaels?" His throat felt dry and raw.

"She's in ICU also."

He relaxed. She was okay.

"Your family is here and anxious to see you. I'll bring them in, but they can only stay for a minute. You need your rest."

She left quietly and Marisa ran in and grabbed him. He gripped her tightly and felt her tears on his face. And his own.

"I'm so happy you're alive. It's been so terrible thinking you and Cari were…"

"Shh." He stroked her hair. "We made it."

"Our prayers were answered."

"How's Cari?"

Marisa lifted her head, brushing away tears. "Her family is with her and I'm on my way there now. Mother, Father and Daphne are waiting, so I can only stay a minute. I finagled my way in first because I wanted to see Cari, too." She kissed his forehead. "I'll be back later. I love you."

"I love you, too," he murmured as she walked out.

Daphne.

It took him a moment to bring up her face.

His life just got very complicated.

Before he could ponder that issue, his parents arrived. His mother hugged him and tickled his beard. "My precious son, you're so handsome and wonderful to see, even with the beard."

He rubbed it. "It's a bit scratchy. Cari and I are lucky to be alive."

On the other side of the bed, his father gripped his hand so tight Reed thought his bones were going to snap. "We're all so grateful." Richard took a breath. "Son…"

"What?" Reed asked when his father couldn't seem to say anything else.

Richard shook his head. "Nothing. You just get better."

Vanessa stroked his arm. "I baked you cookies."

He frowned, thinking he'd heard her incorrectly.

"In all the excitement I forgot to bring them, but I will tomorrow. You'll be stronger then, too."

"You baked cookies for me?"

"We've all been going through a rough time." His father patted his hand. "Get some rest and we'll talk more later." Richard paused. "Son, I'm glad you're home."

"Me, too."

His mother kissed him again and they left. He lay there feeling disconnected with the world and his family.

He needed to see Cari.

He tried to move, but couldn't seem to make his body work. A delicate perfume wafted to his nostrils and he looked up to see Daphne staring at him. She was as beautiful as ever.

"Oh, darling." She gazed down at him in shock. "What happened to you?"

"A plane crash."

"You poor thing," she cooed, touching his arm in a tentative gesture. She made no move to hug him and he wondered why.

"It's been so horrible." A tear slipped from her eye. "I was so worried and we canceled all the wedding plans."

"You took time to do that?" He was stunned. Did a grieving person think about things like that?

"Of course. I had to do something or break down completely."

"It's over now," was all he could say.

"Yes. Now we can go ahead with our plans."

Plans? He couldn't even think beyond this moment.

"The first thing is to get rid of that beard. It's atrocious."

He loved this woman, didn't he? Where was the emotion, her joy and her love? His mind was just muddled, he told himself. He needed to rest and to regain his strength before he could deal with anything.

"I have to go, darling." She picked up his hand and kissed his knuckles. "I love you. I'll be back tomorrow and we'll talk about the wedding."

"Not tomorrow, Daphne."

Tiny lines marred her forehead. "Oh."

"All I want to do is concentrate on regaining my strength."

"Sure, darling. I'm just glad you're alive."

"Yes."

She kissed his hand again and left.

He closed his eyes and wondered how his life had gotten so messed up. Where did he go from here?

Once again he felt like that little boy who was all alone in the world. For a brief moment in time, though, the most harrowing days of his life, he wasn't alone.

He had Cari.

Closing his eyes, he drifted back to sleep with that thought giving him comfort.

* * *

Cari's eyelids felt so heavy. She was exhausted, but she had to keep up, keep going. Suddenly she sensed something was different and she tried to open her eyes. Through flickers of light she saw she was in a room and not on the dusty, hard ground. Thank God!

Reed had said they were going home. Reed! Where was he? She tried to move but her body was so weak.

Someone touched her face and she looked up into the loving eyes of her mother.

"It's okay, Cari," Ruth said. "You're safe now."

"Ma-ma." Her throat was sore and her lips cracked.

"Shh." Ruth stroked her forehead. "Just rest. You'll feel better soon."

"Where's Re-ed?"

"He's being taken care of."

She turned her head to stare at her father.

"Girl, you're a sight for sore eyes." He bent to kiss her cheek. A scent of Old Spice drifted to her nostrils. His hand shook as he took hers. She felt the calluses that defined exactly who he was—a hardworking man who loved his family.

"Dad-dy."

"You rest. We'll be right outside if you need anything."

Ruth hugged her with trembling arms and Cari wanted to cling and never let go. But she was so tired.

She drifted back to sleep.

She was home.

The next morning Reed was much stronger. They removed the IV and he was allowed to take a shower and shave. His body was scratched and bruised and ached, but he was alive. So was Cari. He planned to see her sometime today.

He had a liquid breakfast and he couldn't seem to get enough fluid. It was strange because he wasn't that hungry. He just wanted water.

The doctor arrived and checked him over. He said Reed was doing well and after an MRI of his head, Reed could go home. Since Reed's head had been injured, the doctor didn't want to miss anything.

Reed didn't have a problem with that. Home. He suddenly realized home was a lonely condo. He could go to his parents' house but that might be cruel and inhuman punishment and he didn't know if he was up for it. He'd never felt more alone in his life.

A nurse came in and checked his vitals and removed his breakfast tray. As the nurse left, Daphne breezed in.

"Oh, darling." He sat on the side of the bed and she hugged him, kissing his face. "You're so much better."

"Yes. I'm ready to leave."

She frowned. "Is that wise? You're still very weak."

"I'm fine."

She kissed him again and her delicate perfume surrounded him. It didn't ignite his senses the way it usually did. It irritated him more than anything. Breathing fresh air for days, he found the fragrant scent offensive. That would change he was sure.

"My mother is going ahead with the wedding arrangements and my dress is being flown in from Paris." She clapped her hands. "I'm so excited. I thought my life was over, but now I have you back."

He swallowed hard and said what he had to. "Daphne, I'm not up to planning a wedding, so please stop the arrangements."

"What!" Her blue eyes narrowed.

"I've just been through a horrendous ordeal and I need time to get my bearings. I hope you can understand that."

"I'm trying." Her bow mouth formed a pout. "How much time do you need?"

"I'm not going to be pressured." The words came out sharper than he'd intended. He took a deep breath. "After cheating death or facing death, however you want to say it, a man takes stock of his life. That's what I'm doing. My view of my life has changed. I have issues with my father and my mother and I know now I have to sort that out. I have to do a lot of things before I can think about a wedding."

"Are you calling off the engagement?" Anger was evident in her eyes and in her voice.

"I'm asking for time, that's all."

She wrapped her arms around him, kissing his neck. "Okay. I love you so much. I can wait."

As she walked out, he wondered what she'd say if he told her he had made love to another woman. Would she still love him? His deceit weighed heavily upon his mind. He'd seen his father deceive his mother for years and he vowed he would never be a man like that. But he was.

That stung.

Something else he had to come to grips with.

Cari woke up feeling refreshed. The fatigue had lifted. The doctor checked her over and said once her bruises, sunburn and blisters healed she would be fine. She was really happy when he said she could take a bath and get cleaned up. He added he would check her again in the afternoon and if everything was okay she could go home.

Her parents had spent the night with Kitty and the three of them were there early. The nurse wheeled her to a large bathroom and helped her into a tub. The water was cool and a solution had been added to help the sting of the sunburn. While her parents waited, Kitty washed Cari's hair and cleaned the dirt from under her nails.

Kitty eyed Cari's bruises. "Are you in pain?"

Cari wiggled her legs in the water. "Right now I'm in heaven." Her body still ached and her blisters burned, but she didn't want her sister to be concerned. Her family had worried enough.

She washed the dirt from her weary body and just luxuriated in the water. Leaning her head back, she thought of the last time she was in water—the gully. In Reed's arms.

They said everyone had fifteen minutes of fame. She wondered if that applied to love. If so, then she'd had more than fifteen minutes of love. And she didn't feel badly about taking that time. She should. Reed was engaged to someone else. All's fair in love and war, though.

"You have a dreamy look on your face," Kitty said, carefully cleaning Cari's nails.

"Mmm." Reed's memory surrounded her and her body was warm and relaxed.

Kitty dipped Cari's hand into the water. "Thinking about someone special? A certain man?"

Cari opened her eyes. "Maybe I'm just happy to be alive."

Kitty looked at her. "Was it awful out there?"

"Yes, but we had each other." She sat up. "Hand me a towel, please." It had been a horrific time, but in its own way it had been magical. She'd had Reed. It would be their last time together. She would treasure that.

Back in the ICU she visited with her parents and they fussed over her. She felt loved. After the nurse attended to her blisters and sunburn, Cari drifted off to sleep.

Reed was ready to go home. He sat on the side of his bed in the jeans, white shirt and loafers his sister had brought him.

"So, where do you want to go?" Marisa asked.

"I'm opting for the peace and quiet of my condo."

"Reed." She sat beside him and looped her arm through his. "Please come to the ranch and stay a few days. The kids would love it and I could see you every day just to reassure myself that you're alive."

"Marisa, to tell you the truth, I'm a little confused at the moment. I guess it's after-effects of the trauma or something, but I'm trying to come to grips with everything that has happened."

She tightened her arm. "This has deeply affected all of us and it has changed Mother and Father."

"What do you mean?"

"Father locked himself in his study and wouldn't come out and when he did he snapped at everyone. Mother was just the opposite. She couldn't let herself believe you were dead. She embraced the Michaels family wholeheartedly and loved Ruth's stories about cooking for her children. That's why she had to bake cookies for you. She had to do something motherly, something that was lacking in her own role as a mother."

"She actually baked the cookies she brought this morning?"

"Yes, and as Ellie said, it was a sight to see."

They laughed together as brother and sister who knew the idiosyncrasies of their parents.

"I have a better idea," Marisa said, her voice excited. "Spend some time with Mother and Father. They'll make sure you have privacy and it may be what you need to heal some of the wounds you have from the growing-up years. It's time to forgive and forget. I did and I know you can, too."

He looked at his beautiful sister. "But you never forget, do you, sis?"

"I do my very best." She smiled brightly. "I

have Ellie, Jack and the man of my dreams. Forgetting is easy. I just have to let myself."

"Then I will, too." He figured it was time to get through all the manipulation and control of his childhood. Once he did that he knew he could sort out the rest of his life. At the moment that was causing him the most confusion.

The rest of his life. He wondered what that was.

Marisa slipped off the bed. "Great. Mother's having a dinner party tonight just for family and we'll all give thanks for seeing your handsome face." She kissed his cheek. "I'll see you then." She pivoted at the door. "If things get too much with the parents, you're always welcome at the ranch."

"I know, sis." He winked. "I'm really old enough to stay by myself."

"But not right now." She stared straight at him with a look that dared him to deny it.

"Okay. Maybe not right now."

"I'm not trying to control you," she added for clarity.

"Never in a million years."

They smiled at each other and Marisa left. Reed eased off the bed and glanced at the clock on the wall, wondering when the nurse was going to bring his release papers.

Soon he would be with his family. And Daphne.

First he had to see Cari.

Chapter Fourteen

Cari and Marisa hugged for a long time.

Finally Marisa drew back. "You look so much better today."

"Conscious and clean I always look better," Cari joked. It was the best she could do, even with her friend.

"How are you?"

Cari managed a smile. "I'm going home this afternoon."

"Where would that be?"

"I'm going to my parents' for a couple of days to recuperate."

"That's good. Your family will enjoy having you."

"Yes, I need them right now." Cari scooted up in bed. "How's Reed?"

"He seems fine. I just left him and he's waiting for Daphne. She's chauffeuring him to my parents'."

Daphne. The other woman. Her stomach tied into a knot.

"Hey. What's that look about?"

Marisa knew her too well, but Cari wasn't ready to share.

"Do you want to talk about it?"

"Not yet," she murmured, and she wasn't sure if she would ever be ready. It seemed ironic that she'd survived to come back to the same old broken heart.

Marisa hugged her again. "When you want to talk, I'm always here."

"I know," she whispered, and tears clogged her throat.

"Your parents have had a profound effect on my mother." Marisa was wise enough to change the subject.

"How?"

"Ruth and Sam came to my parents' house while we waited for updates about the crash. My father was his usual grouchy self, but my mother was quite taken with yours, especially hearing about all the things she does for her children. Ruth taught her to knit and Vanessa insisted on making cookies even after we'd heard the news that there were no survivors."

"Oh." Cari was saddened, but she couldn't let herself sink into that frame of mind. "My parents came to the Preston estate?" She couldn't quite believe that. Her father rarely left the farm.

"Yes. We all needed to be together."

Cari was speechless as she realized what her parents and the Prestons had been through. It was such a relief the tragedy was now over and had a happy ending.

They embraced once more and Marisa left. Cari wondered about life and its twists and turns. She'd survived a plane crash, but how would she survive a broken heart?

A little later two investigators from the National Transportation Safety Board arrived and asked if she was up to talking about the crash. She told them what she remembered about the actual crash, but several of the details had conveniently disappeared from her memory. Tricks of the mind or mind-protecting defense, Mr. Sparks told her. Some things a person just doesn't want or need to remember. Cari felt that was very true.

"Are you up for some hard questions?" Mr. Cober asked.

She swallowed. "Yes."

He flipped on a tape recorder. "You pulled Mr. Preston from the plane?"

"Yes. I could smell fuel and knew we had to get out. I checked Melody's pulse and I couldn't find one." Cari looked down at her trembling hands and she gripped them tightly. "I couldn't get to Fletcher. There was so much wire, metal and debris hanging from the ceiling, and the floor was littered with the contents of the plane."

A slight pause and Cari managed to continue. "Fletcher must have done a great job of trying to handle the plane because it landed almost like on a runway except on the edge of a mountain. The side of the plane was tilted down slightly and the door was flung off so it made getting Reed out easier." She paused. "I dragged him as far as I could and then I sprinted back for Melody. The plane exploded and knocked me backward. And…and…"

Mr. Sparks touched her shoulder. "It's okay Ms. Michaels. We'll talk when you're stronger."

"No." She gathered herself. "I want to tell

you so you can find out what happened for Melody's and Fletcher's families."

"Our findings indicate the plane took several lightning strikes."

"The thunderstorm was growing severe and we could see a lot of the lightning."

"The mountain areas of west Texas, especially the Davis Mountains where we located the remains of the plane, create very large thunderstorms that loom above the altitude that most commercial and private aircraft cruise. Navigating around these storms can be risky and pose the threat of lightning strikes. Under the circumstances, Fletcher did very well controlling the plane. His skill saved your lives."

"But it didn't save his." Her voice was barely a thread of sound and she realized she didn't want to talk anymore.

"You're a very brave woman, Ms. Michaels. You didn't panic. You did what you had to."

"Thank you."

"We'll be in touch."

She nodded as they walked out.

The plane crash was heavy on her mind. She tried to shake it, but she had a feeling it was going to be with her for the rest of her life.

She glanced up and Reed stood there. Her pulse leaped at the sight of him. Shaded honey-colored eyes stared at her and they reflected a shared pain that only they knew about. His hair was neatly combed and a tiny scar marred his sunburned left temple. The clean-shaven lines of his strong face were back.

As was the CEO.

Her boss.

But somewhere in west Texas they had crossed a line that would change their relationship forever. She didn't regret it. She just had to find a way to move forward.

"How are you?" he asked, his voice like velvet against her skin. She trembled from the sensation.

"Fine," was all she could say, though she wanted to ask questions. About Daphne.

"You look much better. I was so worried at the end. Help came just in time."

Her eyes held his and she felt that magnetic pull of the senses. She resisted, as did he.

"Your beard is gone," she said to relieve the tension, but it only seemed to increase it.

She could actually feel the caress of his beard against her bare skin.

"Yes." He rubbed his jaw. "I feel human again."

She bit her lip and fought all the emotions in her. "So do I." She drew in deeply. "I had a wonderful bath this morning."

They were talking like friends, acquaintances. That's exactly what they were. Two acquaintances who had made love in the most amazing way. They had lived in the moment and now they were back in the real world.

Reed cleared his throat. "I'm going to stay at my parents' for a couple of days and I didn't want to leave without saying goodbye."

Goodbye.

Goodbye had a finality to it that she didn't want to hear.

"Did the doctor say when you could leave?"

She swallowed the blockage in her throat. "Probably later this afternoon."

An unbearable silence followed.

"Cari, I know you think you have feelings for me."

Oh, wow. It was going to be one of those "it's not you it's me" kind of conversations. That made her angry.

"I don't think, I know."

"Cari." His eyes pleaded for her to understand. In a small way she did.

"We shared a horrific and magical time out of time. That belongs to you and me and no one else. I'm not asking or expecting one thing from you, so don't try to tarnish what happened with guilty feelings. We didn't know if we were going to live or die, so I think we're allowed to be human."

Reed stared at Cari, a woman who made him stronger just by being in his life, and wondered why he couldn't admit what he felt for her. Maybe because it was tainted with deceit. Or maybe as he'd told Daphne, he needed time to come to grips with what he was feeling.

For Daphne.

And for Cari.

Time would tell if his feelings were real or only a result of their near-death experience. The last thing he wanted was to hurt Cari. He didn't want to hurt either woman.

"I have responsibilities…"

"I know. Don't beat yourself up over this. We have a tomorrow and I'm grateful for that. I know you are, too. I wish you nothing but happiness."

Reed couldn't take his eyes from her face

and the sadness in her dark eyes. She meant every word she was saying. Was she for real? Every woman he'd ever known had always wanted something from him. He was an heir to a fortune and that increased his attraction tenfold. All of his life he had dealt with it and it had always felt like a burden. To Cari it didn't seem to matter. Maybe he'd lost his razzle-dazzle if he'd ever had it, except in her mind.

He took a step farther into the room. "If you need anything—"

"I won't."

He shoved his hands into his pockets. "You're not going to let me finish a sentence, are you?"

"Probably not. I'm in a feisty type of mood." Her eyes shimmered like the west Texas stars and he felt their warmth in places he shouldn't. But it was all he could feel.

"I think in some way I'm always going to be bound to you."

She winced. "Oh, that sounds painful."

"You know what I mean." Their easy banter was coming back. Sometimes it seemed as if they could talk forever.

"Yes, I do."

He stepped a little closer to the bed. Her

skin was sunburned, but he knew it was silky smooth to touch. She was hollow-eyed and thinner, but she still had that intriguing appeal that had always captivated and irritated him at the same time.

Unable to resist, he touched her red cheek. "Thank you for saving my life."

"Consider it part of my job description."

He nodded, knowing why she was being flippant and also knowing he had to get out of this room.

"Take care of yourself and don't worry about coming back to work. Take all the time you need."

Something snapped in Cari. He was treating her like an employee, denying everything they had shared. In his comfortable real world he was back to being Reed Preston and still keeping her at arm's length.

She couldn't hold back her feelings any longer. "I said I didn't expect anything from you, but actually I do."

"Anything." The light in his eyes should have stopped her, but it didn't.

"Be honest. Stop running from the truth. Stop hiding behind honor, duty and commitment. You're afraid—"

"Cari..."

She held up a hand. "Let me finish. You owe me that." She swallowed hard. "Loving someone, like you loved your parents, brought you pain, and you've built a world where you can never be hurt again. Sometimes love hurts, but then it also can bring fulfilling, immeasurable rewards. Please don't stay that lonely little boy. Allow yourself to love with all your heart, even if it's Daphne. That's my wish for you."

They stared at each other for a long moment and then he turned and strolled from the room.

Cari held her hand to her cheek, still tingling from his touch.

The ball was now in his court. He had decisions to make and she prayed he made the right ones. Would he confront his fears and accept love into his life? Would he ever admit he loved her? Or would he take the safe route and marry Daphne?

He was a man of character and she had always known that. It was one of those things she loved about him. For once in his life she hoped safe was not an option for him, not after what they had been through together, after what they had shared.

Brushing away a tear, she turned onto her

side and let them flow freely. She needed to. Maybe in a silent way she was saying good-bye to everything that might have been. As sobs racked her body, she realized some things weren't meant to be.

But accepting that reality would take time. Maybe forever.

An hour later the doctor came in and checked her over. He gave the okay for her to go home. He advised her to go for counseling and she said she'd think about it. The one thing she needed now was her family. She'd spent years dreaming of leaving her small-town roots. Now she couldn't wait to go back.

The doctor then went over guidelines for her diet. So far she'd only had liquids, pudding and soup. He wanted her to slowly add solids back into her diet. He also wrote a prescription for an ointment to be administered to the blisters and sunburn and advised her not to wear shoes for a while. Mostly he wanted her to take life slowly.

That suited her fine. She planned on enjoying every moment as much as she could.

Kitty breezed in with a carryall. "I have get-away clothes."

Cari swung her legs over the side of the bed. "I'm ready."

"I have strict orders to bring you straight home." Kitty unzipped the bag and pulled out jeans and a pink knit top. "Mom is fixing up our old room."

Cari cocked an eyebrow. "I don't plan to stay that long."

Kitty stopped and looked at her. "Please let us pamper you. It's the least you can do after taking ten years off our lives."

"Okay. I'll be very docile."

Kitty laid the clothes on the bed. "Yeah, right? Since when?"

"Since I've learned to be grateful for everything I have."

"Oh, sissy." Kitty hugged her tightly. "It's so good to have you back."

Cari held on for a moment longer. "Me, too. Now help me dress. I might topple on my head."

After she was dressed, Kitty went to check on the release papers. Cari sat in a chair and waited.

Richard Preston walked into the room. Usually the sight of the man tied her stomach in knots. Today her insides were calm. After facing death, Mr. Preston's power took on a whole different meaning. He was just a person, as Marisa had said, and Cari's life or happiness did not depend on him or his company.

"Ms. Michaels," he said. "I'm glad to see you're going home."

She managed a smile. "So am I."

He shoved his hands into his tailored slacks. "I want to thank you for saving my son's life. You will have a job at Dalton's forever."

She wasn't sure how to respond to that and she really wasn't sure about her job, so she replied honestly, "I would have done it for anyone."

He nodded. "I believe you would. You're an exceptional young woman."

Cari was taken aback and she was glad when Kitty returned. "Hey, Mr. Preston," Kitty said. "Doesn't Cari look great?"

"Yes, she does."

Kitty studied him. "You know, if you'd stop by my shop I could put some low lights in your gray hair and it would be stunning. It might help your mood, too."

"I'm satisfied with my own stylist," he replied rather stiffly.

"Relax, Mr. Preston. I was teasing," Kitty told him. "Don't you have a sense of humor?"

"I was born without one."

Kitty drew back. "Now that's just sad."

Cari noticed the corners of his mouth twitch. He had a sense of humor, but he kept it hidden. Watching the whole scene, she marveled at her sister's nerve. She'd had the same nerve, though, when she'd first started at Dalton's.

Suddenly Kitty smiled. "You're putting me on."

"You're so easy," Richard replied. "And sincere. I appreciate the thought." He glanced at his gold watch. "I have to be going. Reed will be home soon. I just wanted to see Ms. Michaels." He glanced at Cari. "Thank you."

She could only nod.

Thirty minutes later a nurse wheeled Cari through the lobby with Kitty trailing behind. Kitty hurried to bring her car around and Cari waited with the nurse. A large TV screen was in the lobby and a news report came on.

"After surviving a plane crash, Reed Preston, Texas heir to the Dalton's Department Stores empire was released from the hospital today," the reporter was saying. The rest of his words went over Cari's head. Her eyes were riveted on Reed and Daphne entering the backseat of a limo. Lightbulbs flashed and Daphne smiled into the camera, waving.

As she watched, that tiny sliver of hope she clung to shattered. Reed had made his choice. He was more comfortable with safe. With his fiancée. Whatever he and Cari had shared was over. Really over. She brushed away an errant tear as the reality of that became very clear.

Only the heartache remained.

Chapter Fifteen

Richard watched Vanessa flutter around the dining table checking to make sure every place setting was perfect.

She repositioned a crystal goblet. "Isn't this exciting? Our son is coming home."

He had to agree. "Yes, it is."

Vanessa glanced at her watch. "They should be here soon and, Richard—" she took a moment to spare him a pointed glance "—I want this to be a happy occasion. No arguments. Just happiness."

He leaned against the door frame. "I was thinking the same thing, and I also think it would be best if I didn't mention my involvement in Reed's engagement."

Vanessa stopped in her perusal of the table. "What do you mean?"

"Telling him is only going to upset him."

"And revealing your sins is not a Richard Preston thing."

He didn't deny her words because they were true. Any guilty feelings he had, he ignored. God wouldn't want Reed hurt was his reasoning. "Life is back to normal and I feel I should leave it that way."

Vanessa's eyes narrowed. "There's just one little problem with that."

"What?"

"You told *me*."

Richard frowned, not believing what she was implying. "Are you saying you'd tell him?"

Her eyes widened, the lights of the chandelier reflected in them. It wasn't a soft light. It was hard as steel.

"We almost lost our daughter, not to mention our darling Ellie, because of our manipulations. We thought our son was dead for days. I've learned a very valuable lesson in all the heartache." Her eyes held his. "Honesty, Richard. All these things have happened for a reason and we have to make amends. We have to be honest with our children. Reed has to know you set up the dinner date with Daphne and then we let him make his own decisions. After that we support him completely."

He straightened from the door frame. "But don't you see, once I tell him, he'll be so angry he'll leave Dalton's and cut us out of his life. Is that what you want?"

"No." She shook her head. "But it's a chance we have to take. If you *don't* tell him and he finds out from someone else, you run the risk of really losing him forever. That's not a risk I'm willing to take."

"Vanessa, be reasonable. How will he find out?"

The steel in her eyes grew harder. "I remember you saying the same thing about Marisa. You said she would never find out about her baby. But she did, didn't she?"

Guilt slapped him in the face then. At that moment, he hated Vanessa for pointing out his faults and his misdeeds.

When he didn't reply, Vanessa went on. "I've never been a big believer in fate, kismet or whatever. I dealt with life my own way, uncaring of others. My father made the world my playground and I selfishly enjoyed every minute of it. Looking back, I can see just how selfish I was. I had children and other people cared for them. I left my son in your care. I should never have done that. He needed to be with his mother and not a ruthless, unfeeling bastard."

Richard flinched from her words but he couldn't deny or defend them. All he could do was stare at her and wonder if she was having a nervous breakdown.

She placed her hands on her hips. "I'm not trying to be mean, Richard. In the same vein I'd call myself an unfeeling, heartless bitch."

"We made mistakes," he said.

"Yes." She nodded. "That's what I'm saying. It's time to prove we're not those people anymore."

He closed his eyes briefly. "I can't lose my son again."

"We have to hope he appreciates your honesty."

"Van—"

"No." She stopped him quickly. "You'll tell him." She linked her arm through his. "But not tonight. This time is for happiness."

As they walked into the living room he knew she was right. He'd promised, but it was hard to keep that promise when life was good. On the other hand, he wasn't sure what would happen if he didn't.

For once in his life he wasn't willing to take that risk.

When Reed arrived at his parents', the NTSB investigators were waiting. They sat in his father's study going over the crash. He told them everything he remembered.

"When no one came to rescue us, we decided to walk out."

"How did you manage?" Mr. Sparks asked.

"We didn't have anything but the clothes on our backs. Some things were scattered down the mountain. Cari saw a backpack and climbed down to get it even though she's afraid of heights. We fly all the time and I never knew she was afraid of heights."

He rubbed his hands together trying not to get sidetracked. "It must have been Melody's. We found water, cereal bars, sneakers, a scarf and things we could use. Cari had lost her heels in the plane and even though the sneakers didn't fit she wore them. We used the water sparingly and a metal file worked to cut into a prickly pear cactus. The file broke easily, but we found the fruit of another cactus to eat."

"You did very well under the circumstances," Mr. Cober said.

Reed eyed the investigator. "You stopped looking for us?"

"Yes. We saw no signs there were any survivors."

"The rain washed away all the evidence I suppose."

"Yes."

Reed thought of something. "I discarded my broken watch on the ground not far from the crash site."

"It wasn't recovered. An animal or bird must have taken a shine to it."

"I suppose." Reed looked back at his clasped hands. "I kept telling Cari we were going to make it, but at times I wasn't sure. She was getting so weak and I was, too. But I wouldn't let it show. I had to be strong for her. That petite woman pulled me from the plane moments before it exploded. I'll never be able to repay her."

"I don't think she wants you to," Mr. Sparks replied. "From what I've seen of Ms. Michaels she's a very strong and competent young woman. She would have done the same for anyone."

She would. That's who Cari was, a person

who gave with all her heart. And she loved him. All she wanted was his unconditional love.

He would never be able to give her that.

Why not?

Be honest, she'd said. *Please don't stay that lonely little boy.*

He shook the thought away.

Reed settled in for an evening with his family. Marisa, Colter and the kids were there and it made everything perfect. With Ellie and Jack around, there wasn't any time for deep introspection. He needed to lose himself in their vitality.

His mother had the cook prepare potato soup for him and he was touched by her thoughtfulness. Although the doctor had said he could slowly add solid food back into his diet he wasn't all that hungry. Not even for the prime rib that was served to the others.

After the maid removed the plates, his father asked, "What's for dessert, Vanessa?"

Vanessa pushed back her chair. "We're not having dessert."

Richard's brows furrowed. "What do you mean we're not having dessert?"

Vanessa reached for Reed's arm, and Reed rose to his feet.

"We're going to the kitchen to make dessert," she announced.

Richard threw his napkin on the table. "You have to be kidding me."

"No, not even close," Vanessa answered, and they all trailed into the kitchen. The servants had conveniently disappeared. Vanessa ordered everyone around the large oak table.

"This is very strange," Daphne whispered to him.

Richard leaned in and whispered in that same hushed voice, "This has been hard on her and I believe she's having a nervous breakdown."

"Don't be silly," Marisa said. "She's just happy her son is alive and she wants to do something for him. Something motherly, so go along with whatever she's planned." Marisa lifted an eyebrow at her father. "Or else."

"Mommy's tough, Grandpa," Ellie spoke up. "You better behave."

Richard winked at his granddaughter. "For you, sweetheart, anything."

Vanessa came back with a white apron over her silk dress. Reed just stared at her. Marisa was right. Their mother had changed or she was having a nervous breakdown as his father had insinuated. But he didn't think so. She seemed to have a need to touch him, to please him, and she'd never been like that before.

"I noticed they were letting you eat pudding at the hospital," Vanessa said to him. "I asked Ruth how to make it and she said I should try something easy and told me what to buy."

"You went to the grocery store?" Richard asked before Reed could.

"Yes, dear, and it's really an interesting place with so many mothers with carts and kids. I just never realized it was a gathering place for mothers."

"They do most of the cooking," Marisa pointed out.

"Yes, and tonight I'm making dessert for my son and everyone else, too."

"Vanessa, I do not want pudding for dessert." Richard made his views clear.

So did his mother. "Well, Richard, you're out of luck. It won't hurt you to skip dessert."

"What!" he spluttered, but Vanessa didn't pay him any attention.

She brought a bowl with several items in it

to the table. Removing the contents, she held up a box. "This is instant chocolate pudding."

"Yay!" Jack clapped. "I love chocolate pudding."

Colter ruffled his son's hair. "Be patient, son."

Vanessa opened two boxes and emptied them into the bowl and added measured milk. "Now watch," she instructed as she whisked the ingredients together. "We let it set for a few minutes and then we'll have pudding. Isn't that amazing?"

"Absolutely." Reed stood and kissed her cheek.

Marisa brought bowls, spoons and napkins. Soon everyone had a bowl of pudding. Jack dived in first. Even Richard took a bowl, mainly because Marisa placed it in front of him.

They sat around the kitchen table like a normal family and Reed felt at home for the first time in his life.

Afterward they retired to the living room for after-dinner drinks. As they sipped wine, Ellie showed them her ballet routine. She danced around the living room to the music of *Swan Lake*. Reed thought how beautiful she was, her slim graceful lines and movements just like Marisa's. He glimpsed a tear in Vanessa's eyes. It was his mother's dream that Ellie continue dancing seriously, but that would be up to Marisa and Colter. Most of all it would be up to Ellie. Everyone knew Ellie was her father's daughter and a cowgirl at heart. She was a championship barrel racer. It would be interesting to see what path Ellie's life would take. Whatever she chose, her parents would support her enthusiastically. So would Reed.

Jack wouldn't be outdone. He wanted to show everyone how he could rope. Colter explained rather patiently that he couldn't rope in the house.

"I'll use a pretend rope then," Jack said, and proceeded to demonstrate everything his father had taught him, his tongue held tightly between his teeth. The expressions on his face were priceless. Of course, Ellie egged him on by pretending to be the calf who was being roped.

They had everyone in stitches, even Richard and Vanessa. Daphne seemed bored with the whole thing. He thought she would have been excited about Ellie's dancing, but she wasn't.

Whatever connection he and Daphne had had, they seemed to have lost it. He knew it was him. He'd changed. Daphne hadn't.

She kissed him briefly. "I really must go. I'm so glad you're home. Have fun with your family and I'll see you tomorrow."

As she walked away, Reed wasn't thinking of Daphne. He was thinking about Cari and her words.

Be honest. Please don't stay that lonely little boy.

"Reed."

He turned to his sister.

"Are you okay?"

"Sure. It's been a long day."

Marisa hugged him. "Then get some rest. We'll see you later."

After Marisa and her family left, his parents went upstairs to bed.

And Reed was alone.

Really alone.

Like he had been so many times in his life.

He didn't want to stay that way. Of that he was certain. Cari was right. He'd slipped back into his world, his comfortable, safe world. That Richard Preston had created for him.

It was time to step up to the plate and take control of his life. Out in west Texas he'd told

Cari he didn't know if running Dalton's was his goal or his father's. Or if he knew the difference.

All his life his goal had been to please his father. Even though Richard had shown him very little attention or love, that goal had never changed. When he'd found out what his parents had done to Marisa, he'd left without any intention of returning. But Marisa had begged him to come home. He had, and stepped into his old mold of pleasing Richard.

As he was doing now.

Be honest.

He took a long breath and slowly made his way upstairs to his room. The words followed him.

Be honest.

He looked out the window, the same window he'd looked out of as a kid. His view was the backyard, the pool, the tennis court. Even though the well-lit yard and everything had been updated, it was still the same as it had been back then.

Was he still the same?

He ran his hands over his face and admitted he was. He was still that same lonely little boy who had never known love. Now that he'd found it, why was he still afraid?

A moan escaped him. He could see clearly that Daphne was safe, had fit perfectly into his world. That's what had appealed to him. She'd never touched his heart or deepest desires, not the way Cari had. Was that what he feared? Sharing all of himself? Everything he was and wanted to be? Was he afraid of the pain that might cause?

Cari had said love sometimes brought pain. He gazed out the window and watched the shadows, hiding, not revealing secret places. His heart was just like that—in shadows, hiding from the pain. He sucked in a breath. He was ready for the light to reveal his inner emotions as he had with Cari. He didn't want to hide from reality any longer. Or hide from love.

Suddenly he wasn't afraid anymore.

He would be honest with himself.

Chapter Sixteen

Cari's family smothered her with attention and love. She didn't object because it felt so incredible to be alive. Since she couldn't wear shoes, she was limited to the house and she was okay with that. She slept in her old bed and enjoyed that sense of being home.

Her baby brother, Chase, was home, too, but she knew he wouldn't be for long. The oil company he worked for had interests all over the world and he'd be jetting away soon. It was nice to visit with him. He was so handsome with his dark hair and eyes and that killer smile.

She was sitting in the swing on the wrap-around porch of the old farmhouse when Chase swept her into his arms.

"Where are we going," she asked, laughing.

"For a ride," he replied, depositing her on the seat of their dad's truck. "It's cotton-picking time and I thought we'd drive around and watch big brother and Dad work."

"Sounds like a plan," she said.

Chase turned the key and the old truck sputtered to life. He shifted into gear. It reminded Cari of all the times she'd driven the truck with Chase and Kitty sitting by her side watching her every move. They had all learned to drive early.

Chase drove down a dirt road, dust billowing behind them, in between fields of cotton. Sammy was operating a cotton picker and he waved to them.

"So how are you doing?" Chase asked and she knew they were all worried about her.

"Fine," she replied. "It's good to be home."

"Nothing like coming home, is it?"

"No. I can't believe how anxious I was to get away from here." The truck hit a bump and Cari held on to the door.

"Me, too. I never wanted to be a farmer." Her brothers were so different. Sammy couldn't envision any other life, but Chase was a dreamer like her.

"I probably would have been if it hadn't been for you."

She'd helped to pay for Chase's college and that was a sore spot with their father. But she had known how Chase had felt and wanted to help.

"I just paid your tuition. You worked a job and made good grades. I was proud of you." She reached over and pinched his cheek. "I still am."

"Ah, sis, you're gonna make me blush."

"Yeah, right. You stopped blushing when you were sixteen and discovered the girls were falling over themselves to date you."

He grinned unabashedly. They came to the end of the field and their dad waved from a tractor as he pulled a trailer filled with cotton. It would soon go to the cotton gin.

They waved, but didn't interrupt. Time was of the essence when cotton was in the field waiting to be picked.

As Chase shifted gears to turn the truck around, she asked, "Is there anyone special in your life these days?"

"Nope. Just my work."

"Me, too."

He glanced in her direction. "Kitty's under the impression you're in love with Reed Preston."

"Kitty has a big mouth."

"Oh, I hit a nerve."

"Yes, little brother, so back off."

"Is there any chance…"

"No. He's marrying someone else. Let's drop the subject."

"Yes, ma'am." He parked at the house. "Tomorrow is Sunday and we're finally going to celebrate Dad's birthday. After that I have to be on the road again."

She made a face. "So soon?"

"Yep. I'm headed to Midland and Odessa." He paused, rubbing the palm of his hand over the steering wheel. "Are you gonna be okay?"

"You bet. Nothing keeps me down for long." She sincerely hoped her teasing words were true. Reed had moved on and so could she. Only time would tell though.

He leaned over and kissed her cheek. "I'm eternally grateful we're celebrating a birthday tomorrow instead of attending a funeral."

She smiled even though she felt a moment of sadness. "Me, too." She chased the sadness away with good thoughts. "Tomorrow I'm eating fried chicken and I can hardly wait."

Chase rounded the truck, swung her into his arms and then carried her up the steps. They laughed the whole way as he pretended she was heavy and could barely stand upright from the enormous weight.

Sunday was everything it should have been a week ago. The women worked in the kitchen and the men sat on the porch drinking beer and talking about cotton, corn and oil prices.

Later, Cari sat with her dad on the porch swing.

He stuffed tobacco into a pipe that had belonged to his grandfather. "We've been blessed."

"Yes."

He lit the pipe and puffed on it a couple of times. She loved that pungent scent. Her dad only smoked the pipe on special occasions and it reminded her of the holidays and of her childhood. A childhood she had thought was lacking because they didn't have the material things of other kids. But they'd had so much more. It had taken a plane crash to make her see that.

She had to tell him.

"Daddy, I'm sorry for all the times I was embarrassed to wear hand-me-down clothes."

"Now, girl, that's nothing to be sorry about." He blew smoke rings in the air. "Kids always want what they can't have."

Adults did, too.

"I know you were upset with me for luring Kitty to Dallas and paying for Chase's education."

He leaned forward, puffing on the pipe. After a moment, he said, "Your mom and I wanted to keep all our children right here under our feet in Hillsboro. That way we could keep them safe and protect them, but that's not very realistic." He studied the pipe. "I wasn't upset with you, but myself. I wanted to give my kids those things."

"Oh, Daddy." She hugged him. "You gave us so much more."

"I don't know about that. The early years weren't good. I wasn't here like I should have been, but your mom was good at holding us together." He brushed tobacco from his jeans. "Letting you take off to Dallas after graduation was almost impossible for me to accept, but I did it because you wanted it so badly. You were always dreaming of a better life."

She rested her head on his shoulder. "I always knew what I wanted, but now I'm not sure about my future."

He patted the hand that rested on the sleeve of his chambray shirt. "Go with your heart, girl. Always go with your heart."

Later they made homemade peach ice cream from peaches in the freezer. For a moment Cari thought about Reed and wished he was here. She'd promised to show him a simpler way of life, but now that wasn't going to happen. He'd made his choice. She tried not to let the thought get her down.

They all sat on the front porch laughing, talking and enjoying the special day they'd been given.

On Tuesday Cari knew she had to return to Dallas and sort out her life. She could only stay a little girl for so long. Judith and her mom drove her to her apartment. Ruth had made enough food so Cari wouldn't have to worry about grocery shopping for a week.

Her mom was hesitant about leaving her, but Cari assured her she would be okay. They hugged tightly. Cari tried very hard not to cry and failed.

Later she roamed around her apartment feeling lonely. She wondered what Reed was doing. To stop such thoughts she washed her sheets and cleaned out the refrigerator. Then she went to her computer. She stared at the screen for a long time. All her life she'd had one goal—to be a success. Could she give that up?

With shaky fingers she typed her resignation letter.

She could no longer work for Dalton's.

Of that she was positive.

Reed had breakfast with his parents and they kept glancing at each other. He knew something was up.

"What are your plans today, son?" Richard asked, sipping his coffee.

"I'm going to check in at the office and reassure everyone that Cari and I are fine."

"Reporters are still snooping around, so be extra cautious. Don't worry about the office, everything is under control."

Reed finished his oatmeal and wiped his mouth with a napkin. "You've been taking care of things?"

"We have top people in place to handle any situation."

That kind of explanation no longer sat well with Reed. He carefully laid his napkin on the table. "It sounds as if I'm not needed."

"Don't be absurd. You're the CEO. You need time to heal from this tragedy."

But Reed wasn't in control. His father was. That's what was bothering him. CEO was a title placed on him by Richard, who was still manipulating things behind the scenes.

"Let's go into the living room," Vanessa suggested.

"Good idea." Richard rose to his feet. "Thelma, we'll have coffee in the living room."

"Yes, sir."

Reed carried his cup with him and waited while Thelma served fresh coffee to his parents.

"Your father has something he needs to tell you," Vanessa said, reaching for a cup on the silver tray.

"Vanessa, I do not need your help," Richard snapped.

"What's this about?" Reed asked, knowing in his gut that it was big. After his thinking last night, he had some things to say to his father, but now he had to hear what was so important.

Richard took a sip of coffee and placed his cup back on the tray. "It's about the dinner party where you met Daphne."

"Yes, Mother needed an extra person to make up the seating."

Richard glanced at Vanessa and didn't say anything.

That feeling in his gut intensified. "That's what it was, wasn't it?"

Richard swallowed nervously. "When we were notified there were two survivors found from the crash, I prayed that if God let one of them be you, I would never manipulate your life again. And…and I would tell you the truth."

"About what?"

"The dinner party."

Reed gripped his cup, and Cari's words came back to him. *Daphne was handpicked by your father.* Had she been right?

Richard cleared his throat. "I met Daphne a week earlier at Clyde's office. After she left, Clyde and I were talking about what a perfect couple you'd make, so—" he rubbed his hands together "—we planned to set you up at the dinner party."

Reed carefully placed his cup on the tray before he broke it into a million pieces. "Mother was in on it, too?" he managed to ask through gritted teeth.

"No," Richard replied. "That's what made

it perfect. We all know what an unexpected guest does to your mother and her arrangements. I casually mentioned you could fill in."

"And it worked." Reed rose to his feet because he couldn't sit still any longer. "Goodhearted Reed helps out his mother, and his father stabs him in the back. That sounds about right for the Preston family."

His words were angry, but most of them were directed inward. He knew his father and should have known what was going on. Cari had. Why hadn't he?

"You fell in love with Daphne," Richard pointed out. "I had nothing to do with that."

Reed shook his head. "Oh, you had everything to do with that. Ever since I was a kid I've wanted your approval, your attention and your love. But what I got was a strict regime of how I was supposed to act because I was Richard Preston's son. I was never allowed to be a normal kid, and let me tell you, opening presents on Christmas morning with the nanny sucked." Words seemed to fly out of his mouth of their own volition and made very little sense.

Richard frowned. "We were there."

"Mother was still asleep and you were on

the phone in your study. Marisa and I had Christmases alone and then came the big breakup and I found out what alone really meant. So if being Richard Preston's heir is supposed to mean something special, it doesn't. And I'll tell you something else…it doesn't mean a lot out in west Texas either. You always told me I wasn't ordinary, but out there I was, and pain and suffering showed no discretion."

"Son—"

Reed held up a hand. "I'm getting side-tracked. Let me finish. You say I fell in love with Daphne and you're right. Or I let myself believe she was what I needed in my life. I never stopped to ask myself why she was suddenly there. And I should have." He looked directly at his father. "I think you and I both know why you felt a need to interfere in my life. Suddenly everything seems so clear." Finally the fog had lifted and he saw what Cari had.

"What are you talking about?"

"Cari Michaels," he said without taking a breath. "You knew my interest in her was more than friendly and you had to do something before I married someone so unsuitable.

Even though you promised Marisa and I you would not interfere with our lives again."

Richard paled. "I'm sorry, son. I can see I was out of line. That's why I'm telling you the truth now."

That had Reed. Richard never apologized. He was always right.

Reed ran both hands through his hair and the anger at himself, at his father, slowly ebbed. He'd been through too much to let anger take root, and he could see he was also at fault.

"I'm to blame, too. I could have walked away that night after the dinner party, but I was looking for something and I found it in Daphne."

"You mean…"

"No." He shook his head. "I needed someone to take my mind off Cari. In a small way I suppose I was still looking for your approval. At thirty-six and living through a traumatic experience I can honestly say I don't need your approval anymore." As he said the words, he felt a freedom he couldn't explain.

His father was stone-faced.

"Oh, Reed." His mother wiped away a tear. "I'm sorry about your childhood, but I didn't know how to be a mother."

"Don't worry, Mother. I survived that, too."

Before he could say anything else, Daphne swept into the room.

"This isn't a good time," Richard said, getting to his feet.

"It's the perfect time," Reed corrected.

Daphne glanced from one to the other. "What's going on?"

"Did you know our meeting was a setup?"

She frowned. "Setup? What are you talking about?"

"Your father and mine planned the whole thing."

"So what?" She shrugged. "We fell in love. That's all that matters."

"It matters to me, Daphne. I don't like being manipulated."

"It wasn't anything like that, was it, Richard?" She looked at his father.

Richard drew a long breath. "It was just like that. I wanted Reed to marry someone suitable and I felt I had to do something."

Daphne's eyes grew stormy. "Why did you have to tell him? You're ruining all our plans."

For a full ten seconds there was silence in the room. The writing was on the wall and everyone could see it.

Especially Reed.

He took her hand. "I'm sorry, Daphne. I think you know it's over."

"Reed." Her eyes pleaded.

"I'm sorry if you're hurt and I'm sorry you got caught in the middle of my problems with my father. But I don't believe you're deeply in love with me."

"How can you say that?"

"When I was in the hospital, dirty and with a beard, you could barely stand to touch me."

"You looked so bad and I was just scared."

"It's much more than that. You're in love with Reed Preston the heir, not Reed Preston the man."

She lifted an eyebrow. "Aren't they the same?"

"No. Reed Preston the man is very ordinary and there's nothing ordinary about you."

"Reed, you're not making sense. You need to see a psychologist."

"I'm fine, really," he assured her. "For the first time in my life I'm certain I will be in control of my future."

"Reed."

He hugged her briefly. "I wish you all the best. Keep the ring. It suits you." He strolled toward the stairs.

"Reed," his father called.

He stopped to face him.

"May I ask where you are going?"

"No, you may not, but I will tell you I know what I'm going to do for the rest of my life."

"That would be?"

"I'll let you know when my plans are finalized." He took the stairs two at a time, not looking back.

Chapter Seventeen

Reed hurried to his room, grabbed some money and called a cab. He then told the guard at the gate to let the cab in when it arrived. As he waited, he thought of all he'd learned about himself last night and this morning. Cari had been right. He'd been looking for damage control, as she had put it, and he'd found that in Daphne.

He wasn't sure what that revealed about himself, but he knew one thing. He was scared to death of love. From the start, he'd known Cari had the power to change him. That's what he was afraid of—that power. He'd built a safe little world for himself where exposing his emotions wasn't required. If he did that, it would open him up for pain, and he was an expert at protecting his heart.

Except when it came to Cari.

She seemed to know him better than he knew himself.

He stared out at the bright September day and felt as if his life was just beginning. So many times he wondered what he was going to do with the rest of his life. Now he knew and it was clear as the day.

A week ago he would have been so angry at his father's manipulation. Maybe he wasn't angry because it revealed Reed's own weakness. No one forced him to date Daphne. He'd done that on his own.

He ran his hands over his face. Even though he didn't want to hurt Daphne, he felt there wasn't any other way. He really believed she wasn't hurt as much as disappointed. In the future he prayed she would find someone more suitable for her.

The yellow cab appeared up the driveway and Reed sprinted for the back stairs. He walked through the garages to the driveway and slipped into the backseat. Within seconds, he was headed for his condo.

* * *

Cari had an introspective kind of day. Now that she'd burned her bridges at Dalton's, she had to think about her future. Ever since her childhood she'd dreamed of having a better life. She'd accomplished that goal. Her goal now was to be happy. After what had happened, that was more important to her than anything.

Without Reed she wondered if that was possible.

She shook off that feeling and went to her computer. Tomorrow she'd have to see about getting a new laptop. Her old one was burned to a crisp somewhere in west Texas. She also had to get a new driver's license and new credit cards. But today she needed to work on a résumé. She knew just about everyone in the business and she thought she would apply at several places, but first she'd try Neiman Marcus.

Halfway through the document she had to stop. She couldn't finish it. She felt a betrayal to Dalton's that she couldn't explain. Going into the kitchen, she grabbed a bottle of water out of the refrigerator. She seemed to be thirsty a lot. Maybe her body was still trying to replenish after the dehydration.

She tried not to think about Reed and found that almost impossible. He was still hiding behind duty and honor and running from his feelings.

How could he deny what he felt for her? What they'd shared? They'd made love like there was no tomorrow, both weak and exhausted, but one touch, one kiss and they were energized, needing each other much more than water. She'd always remember that and she had a feeling he would, too.

But would it matter?

Reed didn't go into work as he'd planned. Since he'd missed the memorial services for Fletcher and Melody, he visited with their families. They asked a lot of questions and he answered them as best as he could. He felt it gave them some measure of peace. It also helped him.

Later, he went back to his condo. He didn't sleep much. The crash, life and his future weighed heavily on his mind. By morning he had everything sorted out. He knew what he had to do.

He got out of his car in the parking garage and walked to the executive elevator with confidence. Today marked a new beginning. A new era.

For Dalton's—and for Reed Preston.

Homer hugged him and asked about Cari. He told him she was still with her family. Reed wanted to call, but he thought he'd wait until she had returned to Dallas. Then they would talk.

Everyone shook his hand and said how glad they were he was alive. After the greetings, he went straight to his office, his secretary following him.

"Adele, please tell Jim Kimball I want to see him as soon as possible."

"Yes, sir."

"Also have Monica come in."

"Yes, sir. Anything else?"

"That's it for now."

She handed him an envelope. "This came by courier."

"Thank you."

Adele turned, and then pivoted around. "It's wonderful to have you back."

He grinned. "It feels good, too."

After she left, he looked down at the letter and ripped it open. *A resignation letter from Cari.* His heart dropped like a stone to the pit of his stomach. Had she given up on him?

Monica tapped at the door and walked in. "Reed, I'm so happy you're safe."

In a split second he collected himself. "Thank you."

Reed leaned back in his chair. He'd decided to start his new life by ferreting out the person feeding his father information. Only two people knew his every move, Adele and Monica.

For years he'd been willing to let it slide, but not anymore. To run Dalton's he had to be in total control.

He glanced at Cari's resignation. She had always instilled in him a need to do the best job he could. She gave him strength and courage just as she had in west Texas. He couldn't imagine running Dalton's without her by his side, nor could he imagine a life without her in it.

First he had to take care of business.

By process of elimination he settled on Monica. Adele was very efficient, but she didn't have any deceit in her. He could be wrong, but he didn't think so.

His eyes caught Monica's. "As of today you are no longer employed by Dalton's."

"Excuse me?" Her eyes narrowed to mere slits. "I'm your personal assistant and I demand to know why you're terminating my employment without reason."

He leaned forward, his eyes never leaving hers. "Because you're feeding my father information. He keeps tabs on me through you."

"That's not true. I would never—"

"It's true," he said in a strong voice. "You know it and I know it, so just admit the truth. If you do, I'll give you a good severance package. You keep lying and the offer is off the table."

She chewed on her lip, weighing her odds, and he knew his hunch was right. "Your father is a very powerful man."

"And you thought you'd work both sides of the fence."

She paled visibly. "He said he'd fire me."

That was Reed's point. Richard shouldn't have the power to fire anyone. Reed was CEO and in charge, not Richard. That was going to change.

"I'm sorry, but I can't have someone working for me who I can't trust."

"I am sorry, Reed."

"I know. Next time don't sell your principles for a few extra dollars."

She nodded and walked out.

It didn't make Reed feel any better that he'd

been right. Monica was a good employee and they worked well together, but as he had told her, he needed people on his team who he could trust.

He trusted Cari. But he couldn't allow himself to think about her right now.

Adele buzzed through to let him know Jim Kimball had arrived.

Reed stood and shook the man's hand. Jim had worked as an attorney for Dalton's since he'd graduated from law school. He was now senior attorney for the store and very loyal to Richard.

"Reed, it's so good to see you. You had us all worried."

"Thank you, Jim. I'm happy to be alive. Have a seat."

Jim sat in the leather chair across from Reed's desk. "What's this about?"

Reed came straight to the point. "I want to see my grandfather's will."

"Pardon me?" The man seemed genuinely puzzled. And nervous.

"You're not hard of hearing, are you, Jim?"

"No, sir."

"I expect it in my office in an hour."

Beads of perspiration popped out on Jim's

forehead. He reached in his pocket for a hand-kerchief and dabbed at them. "I don't think I can do that in an hour."

"One hour, Jim."

"Yes, sir." Jim rose to his feet.

"Please don't make the mistake of calling my father. You will be unemployed the moment you do. Am I clear?"

"Yes. It's just—"

"I know you're loyal to my father, but he's not steering this ship anymore. I am, so choose your loyalties carefully."

"I'm close to retirement and I don't want to do anything to jeopardize that."

Reed stood. "It's up to you, Jim. Who are you working for?"

Jim dabbed at his forehead again. "I'll see you in an hour."

"Thank you. Your job is secure. You have my word."

Jim shook his head. "I hope you know what you're doing."

Reed was. He just needed a little extra incentive, and he felt his grandfather's will would give him that. He wanted to read with his own eyes Harold Dalton's plans for the store his father had started.

* * *

Cari took her nieces, Judith, Janice, her sister-in-law, Kitty and her mother shopping at Dalton's. She wore flip-flops Kitty had bought her. She'd promised to take them, but it was difficult. Her family didn't know about her resignation and she wasn't ready to tell them. She didn't want them to worry.

Since the employees knew her, it was an extra-special trip. She wanted to go up to the executive offices, but she didn't. For the first time she didn't want to see Reed.

After everyone had left, Kitty drove her to Melody's parents' home. The memorial service had already been held and Cari wanted to offer her condolences in person. Fletcher's parents lived in Oregon and she had talked to them on the phone, but she stopped by his ex-wife's.

The visits were draining and Cari was glad when Kitty lingered after driving Cari home. She needed the company. They settled in the living room, Cari with her water and Kitty with a cola.

She found herself telling her sister about the ordeal she'd been through, the first time she'd really opened up. Once she started she couldn't seem to stop talking.

"You resigned!" Kitty sat straight up in the chair, appalled at that.

"Yes. I can't work with Reed any longer."

Kitty took a swig of her cola. "I never figured you for a coward, big sister."

"I'm not a coward," Cari retorted. "If you say that again I'm going to pour that cola over your head."

Kitty grinned like a Cheshire cat. "That's the Cari I know and love."

"This isn't easy and I didn't make the decision lightly. It's time for me to move on."

Kitty lounged in the chair. "You're making it easy for Reed."

"Maybe."

"You know." Kitty twisted her hair around one finger. "When we were at the Preston house, I got to know Mr. Preston a little better."

"Yes, I could tell from the way you talked to him the other day." That had surprised Cari because Richard Preston opened up to no one. A trait he'd passed on to his son.

"He's powerful and knows it and he can be intimidating, but the thought of losing his son was tearing him up. It made him human and I felt sorry for him."

"You're probably the first person to ever say that."

Kitty grinned. "Since men now frequent beauty shops, I'm used to dealing with the cranky ones." She winked. "Mr. Preston thinks highly of you."

Cari stared at her baby sister. "What?"

"He knows your contribution to Dalton's has been invaluable. He said he didn't think you were afraid of anything. You stand up to board members and even him when you think something is right for Dalton's."

"He said that." Richard Preston must have been feeling very low.

"Yes. He admires you."

"Let's don't go that far." Cari gave a fake laugh. "He wants me as far away from his son as he can get me."

Kitty lifted an eyebrow. "Are you're going to let that happen?"

Cari closed her eyes and leaned her head against the sofa. She'd always been a fighter. Was she giving up? Hell, no. But she wasn't waiting for Reed any longer.

Liar, resounded in her head like a cymbal. She ignored it.

The doorbell rang. Kitty opened the door to Marisa and they made hot-fudge sundaes and talked about girl things. Reed's name wasn't mentioned.

Before Marisa left, Cari told her she'd resigned from Dalton's. She didn't want Marisa to hear that from anyone else. As always, Marisa understood.

But Cari was beginning to wonder if *she* did.

In less than an hour Jim was back in Reed's office and laid a document in a leather folder in front of him.

"Thank you, Jim. I'll get it back to you as soon as I can."

"Sir, I'd rather take it with me and put it back in the vault. Your father..."

Reed folded his hands across the document. "I'll get it to you as soon as I can."

Jim inclined his head and walked out.

He took a moment to marvel at the fear his father had instilled in his employees. Reed didn't want his employees to fear him. Loyalty, honesty and dedication were what he wanted. That's the way he would run Dalton's.

He focused on the document in front of him. His grandfather's own words seemed to leap out at him and he became more aware of the legacy that had been passed down to him.

Thirty minutes later he rang Adele and she hurried in.

"Call my parents and tell them I would like to see them in the boardroom at one o'clock. Also, contact my sister for the same meeting."

"Yes, sir."

As she made to leave, he stopped her. Picking up Cari's letter, he handed it to her. "Draft a letter stating Cari Michaels's resignation has been accepted and I'll sign it."

"Uh…" Adele seemed at a loss for words.

"Something wrong?"

"Ms. Michaels isn't coming back? Oh, I'm sorry. That's none of my business." She quickly collected herself. "I'll draft a letter right away."

As he saw the fear in Adele's eyes, he felt the power his father was so fond of brandishing. Unlike Richard, though, causing that fear was not a power play or a turn-on for him.

He looked at his secretary. "Adele, it's okay to be sad that Cari won't be coming back. Things are changing at Dalton's and Cari will no longer be vice president. Other changes are to come. I'll get with you on a memo later today."

"Oh. Okay." Adele relaxed, although she seemed eager to escape to her office.

Reed twisted his gold pen between his fingers. He could see Cari's face so clearly and hear her voice. *Junior, what do we do now?* He took a long breath. They accepted their future. To do that he had to let her go because after their ordeal they needed to be free to make the right choices for their lives.

First he had to solidify his future.

Then he would talk to Cari.

Chapter Eighteen

Adele informed Reed his parents were in the boardroom. He picked up his briefcase and headed there. As he took his seat at the head of the table, he glanced directly at his father.

"What's this about, son?" Richard asked. "I have a golf game this afternoon and I'd like to get to it."

Reed glanced at his watch. "Marisa is on her way, so I'd like to wait for her."

Richard's eyebrow shot up. "You asked your sister?"

Before he could reply, Marisa breezed in, kissed everyone and took a seat by Vanessa.

"I hope this isn't going to take long," she said. "I have to be at Ellie's school by two-thirty."

"No, it won't take long," Reed replied.

"What are we doing here, Reed?" Richard asked with a touch of annoyance.

Reed removed the will from his briefcase. "We are the four biggest shareholders of Dalton's and I wanted you to be the first to know of changes that are going to take place."

"You're quitting," Richard said, shaking his head in disgust. "I thought you had more guts than that. I interfered in your life and I apologized, but you're the one who took the relationship to the next level. For heaven's sake, don't throw away your birthright because you're angry at me."

Reed held his father's gaze. "I didn't say anything about quitting. I said things were going to change."

"I promised not to interfere in your life again. Do you want it in writing?"

"Richard, please shut up and let our son talk," Vanessa said. "Everything is not about you."

Richard glared at Vanessa.

"Father," Marisa intervened. "Please just listen to Reed."

Usually Reed would be gritting his teeth by

now. But he felt calm, in control. "For a long time I've been unsure of my life and I've felt like a figurehead here at Dalton's. I've never been in control because—" his eyes caught his father's again "—you manipulate my life, the store, everything behind the scenes."

"I do not. You're the CEO and I've backed away."

Reed didn't even pause. "Monica, my assistant, is on your payroll. You pay her handsomely to feed you information. As of today she no longer has a job."

"Richard!" Vanessa threw up her hands. "I give up. Why can't you let go?"

A scowl appeared on Richard's face.

"It doesn't matter," Reed said. "I'm going to stop it." He tapped the will. "I took time to read Grandfather's will and it cleared away a lot of my doubts."

A look of melancholy crossed Vanessa's face.

Richard's scowl deepened.

Marisa just looked puzzled.

He flipped toward the end of the will. "I'll read Grandfather's wishes in case you've forgotten." He paused. "It's part of a codicil that can be invoked at any time. It reads: 'My first heir has been born, Richard Reed Dalton Preston. He is an heir of my blood and it is my greatest wish that at the age of thirty-five he will take complete control of Dalton's. If he does not wish to do so, then it will fall to my next blood heir. If a blood heir does not wish the responsibility then Richard will continue to run Dalton's as he sees fit and my precious daughter will continue to enjoy the life to which she's accustomed…'"

His voice trailed away and there was total silence.

Richard turned in his chair to face Reed. "I'm not sure what you're getting at. You are in control just as Harold wanted."

Reed closed the document. "No, I'm not, but from this day forward I will have complete control. I'm invoking the codicil. You will back away as you promised when I came to work as CEO. You will no longer be chairman of the board. You will retain a seat, but that's it. People who I can trust will stay in their positions but others will be replaced. This will be a new era for Dalton's." He folded his hands across the document. "Any objections?"

"Not from me," Vanessa said. "I agree heartily."

"Certainly not from me," Marisa added.

Reed stared at his father and waited. The same light brown eyes measured each other. Reed didn't blink or look away. This is where he made his stand.

The scowl on Richard's face eased. "What the hell took you so long?"

Reed didn't move a muscle. "You did."

"Everything I've done I've done with your best interest in mind. I've pushed and pressured you so you could take the heat in the business world. You have to be hard and tough to succeed and I never thought you had those qualities, so I had to be behind the scenes to make sure you didn't fail. As a father that's my role. You may not understand that, but it's the truth."

If his father wanted him to be tough, then he'd show him tough. With a glint in his eyes, he asked again, "Any objections?"

"None," Richard replied. "It's been my dream as well as Harold's that one day you'd take over. That day has come." He stood and held out his hand. "I'm proud of you, son."

Reed shook his hand with strength and confidence. Then Richard did something he'd never done before, he pulled Reed to him and hugged him. "I... I love you, son," came out muffled, but Reed caught it.

His father had never said those words to him and for a moment Reed stood transfixed, almost paralyzed. He let out a long breath and managed to hug his father back. "I love you, too." So many years of tension and three little words absolved a lot of sins.

It definitely was a new beginning. Reed knew that life would not be perfect, but now they would be a family as best as they could.

Marisa hugged him. "I've got to run. Brilliant," she whispered for his ears only and then she was gone. Marisa had her own life and she was happy. That's what Reed wanted now—to be happy.

His mother hugged him also. "I'm proud of you, too. Are you coming back to the house?"

"No, Mother."

She touched his face. "It's your life. You do whatever you want."

"I'm sorry I hurt your feelings the other day about Christmas."

She shrugged. "It was the truth. I'd be the first to admit I was a lousy mother." She wrinkled her nose. "I'm not good at cooking either."

He smiled. "You really don't have to do that."

"Thank you." She sighed with relief. "I'm

actually awful at it. I think I'll leave the cooking to others."

"Hallelujah," Richard said. "I'm going to the club and drinking to that."

"I'll go with you, dear." His mother hugged him again and followed her husband.

At the door Richard looked back. "Good luck, son. Wherever Harold is, he's smiling today."

"Thank you."

Richard hesitated and then added, "For what it's worth, Daphne wasn't the woman for you."

"No, she wasn't, but I know who is."

"Yeah." Richard nodded. "Even though you don't need it, you have my blessing."

"I appreciate that."

Reed gathered his briefcase and headed for his office with a smile.

Richard and Vanessa stepped onto the elevator.

Richard looked around. "Where is that guy who operates this thing?"

"He's probably in the bathroom," Vanessa replied.

"He's kind of funny about this elevator."

"Just push a button."

Richard poked a number. "Our son thought he was going to put one over on me."

"He did," Vanessa told him, reaching in her purse for her compact to check her makeup.

"Yes." Richard had to admit Reed had. "He's a chip off the old block."

"Please." She snapped the compact closed. "I sincerely hope not. I would like my son to have a heart."

He put his arm around her. "Stop being bitchy."

She rested against him. "Do you think Reed will call Cari?"

"I'm not sure."

"It would be nice to have Cari's family over to dinner."

Richard thought about that for a moment. The Michaels family had grown on him, but what he did now would determine his future with his son. The crash had changed Reed. He'd become a formidable man. "No. We will not interfere."

Vanessa laughed softly. "Spoken like a man who has learned his lesson."

"Hear, hear."

In the morning Cari awoke feeling sluggish. She was starting to have nightmares about the crash and she thought she might call a counselor to help deal with it.

Her sunburn was healing and fading to a nice tan, thanks to her olive complexion. Her feet were also healing and she decided to try wearing heels with a back strap. She had to do job interviews soon. Her life seemed to be in a holding pattern and she didn't have the strength to change that.

Or maybe she didn't want to.

Her broken heart was about to get her.

The doorbell rang and she went to answer it. A courier handed her a letter and she signed for it. It had the Dalton logo, so she knew where it was from. Her hand shook as she read it.

Her resignation had been accepted.

By Reed Preston.

Her broken heart shattered into so many little pieces that she fought to breathe. She sat on the sofa for a long time just staring at Reed's signature. How could he?

It took fifteen minutes for the anger to set in. How dare he!

She hurried to her bedroom to dress in a chocolate-brown power suit and ecru silk blouse. After sixteen years at Dalton's, she deserved more than a letter. As she felt the adrenaline pumping through her veins she knew she was coming out of the depression or whatever she'd been in.

Just as she reached the door to her garage, the phone rang. She yanked it up.

"Cari, it's Adele. I hope you're feeling better."

She gripped the receiver. "Yes. Thank you."

"If you have time this morning, Reed would like to see you."

Oh, you bet he was going to see her. "I'll be there in less than an hour," she replied.

"I'm looking forward to seeing you."

Cari didn't even take a minute to wonder what the call was about. She had something to say to Reed Preston and she was going to say it to his face.

Chapter Nineteen

Cari's morning was beyond her usual "take two Tylenol" kind. This was a rip-roaring "take no prisoners" type and she did not intend to control her anger, her resentment or her hurt feelings. She'd earned the right to have her say. She wasn't that naive country girl afraid of rejection anymore.

Pulling into her parking spot, she saw her name was still on the marker. That gave her pause. Cari Michaels—Vice President. But she wasn't. She no longer worked for Dalton's.

She shoved the gearshift into park with more force than necessary and grabbed her purse. Her heels *tip-tapped* across the pavement, echoing through the concrete ceiling with a sharp sound.

Almost two weeks ago she'd made this same walk. Two weeks and her whole life had changed. Her goals and her thinking had also changed. But she was still Cari.

She could see Homer's smiling face, his eyes huge at the sight of her.

"Ms. Cari. Ms. Cari, you're back. You're back," he chanted.

She smiled at his sincere expression. "Yes, I'm back." She couldn't tell him she was only here for an in-your-face session with Reed.

"May I hug you? My mama says not to hug a woman unless I ask. Some people don't like it."

"You can hug me all you want."

He enveloped her in a big bear hug and she couldn't hide her smile.

Inside the elevator, he asked, "Do you want me to make Louise fly?"

"That's okay. I'll take the slow trip."

"Good, 'cause Louise has one speed." He pushed a button. "I watched on the news, Ms. Cari, and Mama and me prayed for you and Mr. Preston."

"Thank you, Homer. That was nice."

As the elevator stopped, she hugged Homer

again and stepped off. She took a moment and absorbed this place that was her second home. The extra-wide hall with Dalton and Preston family photos, the shiny hardwood floors and an ambience that was unequaled in style and class.

She started for her office to say hi to Heather and stopped short. Reed came out of his large office at the end of the hall. He was talking to someone she didn't recognize. Maybe it was her replacement.

He turned and their eyes met. Looking into his warm eyes all her anger and her resentment faded away. A tiny scar was still visible on his left temple, a small reminder of the crash. But she remembered so much more; a man sharing his inner feelings and opening up his heart. To her. She also remembered his touch, his gentleness and his strength. Now at nights when she stirred from a restless sleep she instinctively reached for him. When her hands touched an empty space she felt a loneliness that was hard to take.

Oh God, she loved him. A lot of things had changed, but that hadn't. And just like that, all her anger disappeared.

He walked toward her with an easy athletic stride. "Cari, how are you?"

His voice wrapped around her like a warm comfy blanket. She wanted to snuggle into him and feel that warmth forever. She pulled herself up quickly. How could she be so weak?

She tightened her grip on her purse strap. "I'm fine. I got your message." At the thought of his message some of her anger returned. "I don't have a lot of time. I have job interviews scheduled."

He seemed taken aback. "You're looking for work?"

"Yes. I tried starving and I really didn't like it."

"Cari." He took a step toward her.

"Mr. Preston," the young man she didn't know spoke from behind him. "The meeting is ready to start."

"Thank you." Reed turned to the man. "Brian, this is Cari Michaels."

"Yes, I know." He shook her hand with a firm clasp. "It's a pleasure to meet you."

"And, Cari, this is Brian Parks, my new personal assistant."

New personal assistant? What had happened to efficient Monica?

Before she could ask, Brian said, "Sir, everyone is seated."

"I'll be right there," Reed replied.

"You're busy so I'll just go." For whatever reason he wanted to see her, it really didn't matter. He probably just wanted to talk about a severance deal. Her time here was over. As she'd told Kitty it was time to move on. Now she had to do it with dignity.

"No," Reed said. "I would like for you to attend the meeting."

She was disconcerted. "I don't—"

He looked into her eyes. "Trust me."

When he looked at her like that, she'd follow him anywhere, which she did, right into the boardroom. Everyone stood and embraced her and shook her hand. She'd talked to several of them on the phone and they'd all sent cards and flowers, but it was good to see them in person. She worked with these people every day and it was hard to leave them. She'd never realized how hard until this moment.

After the pleasantries, everyone took their seats. Cari noticed someone was sitting in her chair, obviously the new vice president. She also noticed there were several new faces on the executive team.

She was about to turn and leave, thinking this really wasn't the place for her, when Reed said, "Cari, please sit here." He pointed to the chair on his right. With everyone watching she had no choice. He said to trust him and that's exactly what she did. By now she realized something was afoot, so she eased into the chair and waited.

"Thank you for coming," Reed started to speak. "As all of you know this is a new beginning for Dalton's, a changing of the guard so to speak."

What was he talking about? New beginning? He had her full attention.

"As of yesterday, Richard Preston no longer has any say in the running of Dalton's. I have taken over the reins completely as CEO and chairman of the board. Those people who were loyal to my father and who he paid for information are now gone."

Holy cow, was all Cari could think. She hadn't talked to Marisa in a couple of days and she had no idea this was going on. Even though Marisa was her good friend, it was hard to talk about Reed and the store. She did wonder, though, how this had come about.

"You see new faces on the executive team and I'd like to introduce them and their jobs."

The back of Cari's feet began to hurt. As Reed talked, she slipped one shoe off and then the other. She wiggled her toes and her feet felt better.

"George Ortell will now be vice president. You all know George. He's been a very loyal employee."

George had her job. This was a little too much and she refrained from sending George daggers with her eyes. Reed said to trust him, but she was finding that a little difficult.

"The only position left is that of president. This person will work very closely with me and I was very particular about who this individual would be. Only one person knows Dalton's as well as I do." He paused and his eyes caught hers. "Cari Michaels will be the new president of Dalton's."

What! What did he say?

With her foot, she frantically searched for her shoes beneath the table. But they kept eluding her. So she plastered a smile on her face and wondered if she was dreaming.

The double doors opened. A white linen–covered cart with champagne and hors d'oeuvres was wheeled in. A waiter popped the cork and poured the bubbly.

Reed raised his glass. "I'm looking forward to working with all of you. Here's to a year of change and may it be a big success."

Everyone echoed his sentiments and enjoyed the moment. Cari gave up on finding her shoes and joined the others, without shoes once again.

Soon the cart was wheeled away and the last person filed out. Reed closed the doors with a significant gesture. They were alone. She sank into a chair. Tears filled her eyes and she didn't bother to hide them.

"Hey." Reed pulled a chair close to her. "What is it? Do your feet hurt?"

"A little, but that's not it." She brushed away tears with the back of her hand. "I've just had my dream job handed to me and I should be happy, but I'm not."

Reed swallowed visibly. "Why aren't you?"

She brushed away more tears. "Because I can't accept it."

"Why not?"

"I can't work that closely with you. I'm sorry, but I love you. I just can't see you every day knowing you're married to someone else." She jumped to her feet and hurried for the door.

"Cari."

She stopped and she hated herself for that weakness. *Keep walking.* Somehow she couldn't make her feet move.

"Cari, look at me."

"I just need to get my shoes and purse," she said, turning and avoiding eye contact.

"Will this change your mind?"

She stared at the black velvet box, and the most beautiful diamond she'd ever seen winked back at her. She was immediately better. "What…about… Daphne?" she spluttered.

"We broke up." Then he told her an amazing story. She had to close her mouth several times.

"So you see you were right. My father handpicked Daphne and I was looking for someone to take my mind off you. That doesn't put me in a very good light, but all I can say is that deep down I was trying to please my father. I guess that little boy who yearned for his love and attention resurfaces every now and then. Luckily I'm finally my own person. My own man."

Unable to resist, she touched his face, "I rather liked the old one, too."

Taking her hand, he said, "Cari Michaels, I've never said this to another woman. I've never been able to say it. Being Reed Preston, it didn't seem to be required." He paused and looked down at the ring in his other hand. He raised his eyes to hers. "I love you. Will you marry me?"

She flew into his arms, throwing her arms around his neck. "Yes, yes, yes!" she said, kissing his face over and over.

He held her face with one hand and stared into her eyes a moment before he captured her lips completely. The kiss went on and on, each taking and giving what they needed after being apart for so many days.

Finally Reed pulled her to the chairs and they sat side by side, much as they had sat for days in west Texas. He removed the ring from the box, slipped it easily onto her finger and kissed it.

"I love you," he whispered, looking deep into her eyes. "I'm sorry it has taken me so long to realize that and to accept it. I had to deal with my dysfunctional life before I could tell you, before I could fully share a life with you."

She stroked his face. "I was going to give you an earful for accepting my resignation."

He lifted an eyebrow. "You didn't realize I had a devious plan."

"You don't have a devious bone in your body."

"I don't think I can be Harold Dalton's

grandson and Richard Preston's son and not have a touch of it."

"You handle it with heart, though."

"So you're not upset with me for surprising you?"

"Mmm." She glanced down at her beautiful ring. "Since it came with an I love you and a ring, I forgive you."

"I thought Marisa might have mentioned what was happening."

"Marisa is a very smart lady and she doesn't want to be caught in the middle of our relationship."

"She's very wise and discreet."

Cari couldn't take her eyes off the ring. For days she'd been so depressed, but now their future shone as bright as the diamond.

She could feel Reed watching her. "It's a platinum round cut and it belonged to my grandmother. If you don't like it, we—"

"Your grandmother's?" she asked in an incredulous tone.

"Yes. My grandfather had impeccable taste, but if it's not to your liking—"

"Are you kidding?" She held her hand to her heart, knowing he'd put a lot of thought into the decision to give her the ring. "It's the most beautiful ring I've ever seen and you're not getting it off my finger—ever."

He gently kissed her lips and she smiled into his warm eyes. "I'm glad you like it. It was just sitting in the vault and I thought it was perfect for you."

"It is. It fits perfectly." She stretched out her fingers.

"I noticed."

"Two engagements in one year," she teased. "That's a record even for razzle-dazzle Reed Preston."

He just grinned and she threw her arms around his neck. "I will treasure this ring forever. I will treasure you."

He kissed her cheek, her ear. "I had to go through hell to realize heaven was at my fingertips. I love you."

"I love you, too."

They kissed deeply and after a moment came up for air. "If and when we decide to have children, I sincerely hope we do a better job than my parents."

"You can count on it." She kissed his nose. "We will be hands-on parents and our Christmases will be wonderful. I promise."

"They will be as long as you're in them." He rose to his feet and reached for her hand, pulling her to his side. "Why don't we go up-stairs to the apartment and practice creating the new heir."

She feigned surprise. "Are you trying to seduce me?"

"Absolutely."

"Just wanted to make sure," she replied impishly and wrapped an arm around his waist.

They strolled from the room. At the door Cari stopped. "My shoes."

"Leave them. You should rest your feet and you won't need them for the next twenty-four hours."

"Oh, I like the sound of that."

They kissed again and held on to each other. Cari knew that nothing would ever be as perfect as this moment. Razzle-dazzle Reed Preston was never going to lose his shine. She'd found her prince.

And he loved her.

Epilogue

One year later...

Reed steered the tractor like a pro through the cotton fields toward the Michaelses' farmhouse. Willie Nelson played on the radio and Reed tapped his foot.

"You really like driving this thing." Sam stood beside him just in case Reed had any problem with the clutch and gears. But Reed had it mastered.

"It's relaxing, even with the bumps."

Sam removed his Cowboys baseball cap and scratched his head. "A lot of people don't understand that."

Reed pulled up to the house and turned off the big motor. "You have a believer in me." He opened the door of the air-conditioned cab and climbed out. Sam followed and they strolled to the house.

In the kitchen Cari and her mother were finishing the dishes. Reed took a moment to stare at his wife. Her dark hair was longer, swaying around her shoulders; her eyes brighter and her figure fuller. In early December their first child would be born. Motherhood suited his wife. She actually glowed and he never grew tired of looking at her.

They'd been married almost a year and it had been the happiest of his life. They had a simple wedding with family in a country church in Hillsboro, much to his mother's chagrin. Vanessa brightened when they let her host a big engagement party at the Preston estate. That way both families were content.

Reed slipped his arms around Cari's growing waist and kissed her neck. "How's my lady?"

"Wonderful." She turned in his arms and his heart melted at the glow in her eyes.

"How's little Junior?" They knew the baby was a boy.

Cari looked down. "He's trying to kick

through my stomach. I think he's going to take after his grandfather Preston."

"Bite your tongue." Reed couldn't help but smile though. This child was going to be born with so much expected of him. The next heir. Reed resolved to raise his child quite ordinarily with many days spent here at the farm. "What he needs is ice cream." He headed for the freezer and the homemade ice cream.

"I can't believe you spent all morning churning that old ice-cream maker." Ruth reached for bowls in the cabinet.

"Especially when we have an electric one." Sam eased into a chair at the table.

"My husband loves being a kid." Cari rubbed his back as he scooped peach ice cream into bowls.

Reed couldn't resist a bite. "This is the best stuff. It's worth the extra effort."

Ruth got a phone call from someone at their church and Reed and Cari carried their bowls to the front porch and sat in the swing.

"Happy?" he asked her.

"Ecstatic." She swallowed a mouthful. "I love watching your excitement over simple things."

"I love just watching you."

They smiled at each other and this was

what Reed had wanted all his life—love. He'd finally found true happiness. In his heart he knew he'd never be alone again. He had Cari and she made his world complete.

The crash still affected their lives. He had severe headaches from time to time and Cari had occasional nightmares. They were flying again; their jobs required it. It hadn't been easy and they always flew together. With the baby coming he knew there would be adjustments. They would handle them together and make the right choices.

They were making a nursery in the apartment above the corporate offices. Cari planned to continue working, but she wanted the baby close. He did, too. He was looking forward to fatherhood. Their lives had changed so much in a year.

He glanced at her beautiful face and noticed the tiny lines between her eyes. "Are you remembering?"

"A little." She licked her spoon. "The plane crashed one year ago today."

He kissed her cheek. "And we found each other. I'm wondering if that would have ever happened if not for the crash."

"Yes," she stated. "We were meant to be together."

He gazed into her eyes. "I love you and—"

His phone buzzed, cutting him off. He groaned. He knew who it was. He placed his bowl on the floor and reached for his cell on his waist. "Hello, Mother."

"Reed, darling, are you and Cari coming to dinner?"

"Not tonight. We're at Cari's parents'."

"Oh. May I speak to Cari?"

Reed handed Cari the phone with a raised eyebrow. He heard Cari's part of the conversation and knew what his mother was asking: had they decided on a name for the baby.

He gave Cari a thumbs-up sign to go ahead and tell his parents.

"Dalton Samuel Reed Preston," she said clearly and placed the phone to his ear.

He listened to his mother's excitement for about five minutes before he said he had to go. "We have a busy schedule next week, but we'll try to make dinner one night," he promised before clicking off.

Cari scooted closer and he tucked her into his side. "I take it she's excited."

"Very." They had discussed endless names. One name had stuck in their minds. Boy or girl it had to be Dalton.

Cari rubbed her stomach. "Do you think

there's a chance our baby will grow up normal?"

He squeezed her gently. "With you for a mother he'll be fine. I'll be fine, too. I just have to remember that when my parents are bugging us."

Two trucks drove up in a cloud of dust. Two boys on a four-wheeler emerged through the dust, followed by Judith's girls on another wheeler.

"Sammy, Judith and the kids have arrived," Cari murmured.

"They sensed we have ice cream," Reed replied as Ruth and Sam walked out to join them.

Reed had never been part of a big family and he found he liked it. His arm tightened around Cari.

"I love you, Junior," she whispered. "Forever."

His heart always skipped a beat when she called him that. "Forever," he whispered back.

* * * * *

WESTERN WP PROMISES

YES! Please send me **The Western Promises Collection** in Larger Print. This collection begins with 3 FREE books and 2 FREE gifts (gifts valued at approx. $14.00 retail) in the first shipment, along with the other first 4 books from the collection! If I do not cancel, I will receive 8 monthly shipments until I have the entire 51-book Western Promises collection. I will receive 2 or 3 FREE books in each shipment and I will pay just $4.99 US/ $5.89 CDN for each of the other four books in each shipment, plus $2.99 for shipping and handling per shipment. *If I decide to keep the entire collection, I'll have paid for only 32 books, because 19 books are FREE! I understand that accepting the 3 free books and gifts places me under no obligation to buy anything. I can always return a shipment and cancel at any time. My free books and gifts are mine to keep no matter what I decide.

272 HCN 3070 472 HCN 3070

Name	(PLEASE PRINT)
Address	Apt. #
City	State/Prov. Zip/Postal Code

Signature (if under 18, a parent or guardian must sign)

Mail to the **Reader Service:**

IN U.S.A.: P.O. Box 1867, Buffalo, NY 14240-1867
IN CANADA: P.O. Box 609, Fort Erie, Ontario L2A 5X3

* Terms and prices subject to change without notice. Prices do not include applicable taxes. Sales tax applicable in N.Y. Canadian residents will be charged applicable taxes. This offer is limited to one order per household. All orders subject to approval. Credit or debit balances in a customer's account(s) may be offset by any other outstanding balance owed by or to the customer. Please allow 4 to 6 weeks for delivery. Offer available while quantities last. Offer not available to Quebec residents.

Your Privacy—The Reader Service is committed to protecting your privacy. Our Privacy Policy is available online at www.ReaderService.com or upon request from the Reader Service.

We make a portion of our mailing list available to reputable third parties that offer products we believe may interest you. If you prefer that we not exchange your name with third parties, or if you wish to clarify or modify your communication preferences, please visit us at www.ReaderService.com/consumerschoice or write to us at Reader Service Preference Service, P.O. Box 9062, Buffalo, NY 14240-9062. Include your complete name and address.

REQUEST YOUR FREE BOOKS!

2 FREE NOVELS PLUS 2 FREE GIFTS!

H HARLEQUIN®

SPECIAL EDITION

Life, Love & Family

YES! Please send me 2 FREE Harlequin® Special Edition novels and my 2 FREE gifts (gifts are worth about $10). After receiving them, if I don't wish to receive any more books, I can return the shipping statement marked "cancel." If I don't cancel, I will receive 6 brand-new novels every month and be billed just $4.74 per book in the U.S. or $5.49 per book in Canada. That's a savings of at least 12% off the cover price! It's quite a bargain! Shipping and handling is just 50¢ per book in the U.S. and 75¢ per book in Canada.* I understand that accepting the 2 free books and gifts places me under no obligation to buy anything. I can always return a shipment and cancel at any time. Even if I never buy another book, the two free books and gifts are mine to keep forever.

235/335 HDN GH3Z

Name _____ (PLEASE PRINT)

Address _____ Apt. # _____

City _____ State/Prov. _____ Zip/Postal Code _____

Signature (if under 18, a parent or guardian must sign) _____

Mail to the **Reader Service:**
IN U.S.A.: P.O. Box 1867, Buffalo, NY 14240-1867
IN CANADA: P.O. Box 609, Fort Erie, Ontario L2A 5X3

Want to try two free books from another line?
Call 1-800-873-8635 or visit www.ReaderService.com.

* Terms and prices subject to change without notice. Prices do not include applicable taxes. Sales tax applicable in N.Y. Canadian residents will be charged applicable taxes. Offer not valid in Quebec. This offer is limited to one order per household. Not valid for current subscribers to Harlequin Special Edition books. All orders subject to credit approval. Credit or debit balances in a customer's account(s) may be offset by any other outstanding balance owed by or to the customer. Please allow 4 to 6 weeks for delivery. Offer available while quantities last.

Your Privacy—The Reader Service is committed to protecting your privacy. Our Privacy Policy is available online at www.ReaderService.com or upon request from the Reader Service.

We make a portion of our mailing list available to reputable third parties that offer products we believe may interest you. If you prefer that we not exchange your name with third parties, or if you wish to clarify or modify your communication preferences, please visit us at www.ReaderService.com/consumerschoice or write to us at Reader Service Preference Service, P.O. Box 9062, Buffalo, NY 14240-9062. Include your complete name and address.

REQUEST YOUR FREE BOOKS!
2 FREE NOVELS PLUS 2 FREE GIFTS!

⊞ HARLEQUIN®

Western Romance

ROMANCE THE ALL-AMERICAN WAY!

YES! Please send me 2 FREE Harlequin® Western Romance novels and my 2 FREE gifts (gifts are worth about $10). After receiving them, if I don't wish to receive any more books, I can return the shipping statement marked "cancel." If I don't cancel, I will receive 4 brand-new novels every month and be billed just $4.74 per book in the U.S. or $5.49 per book in Canada. That's a savings of at least 12% off the cover price! It's quite a bargain! Shipping and handling is just 50¢ per book in the U.S. and 75¢ per book in Canada.* I understand that accepting the 2 free books and gifts places me under no obligation to buy anything. I can always return a shipment and cancel at any time. Even if I never buy another book, the two free books and gifts are mine to keep forever.

154/354 HDN GJ5V

Name _____ (PLEASE PRINT) _____

Address _____ Apt. # _____

City _____ State/Prov. _____ Zip/Postal Code _____

Signature (if under 18, a parent or guardian must sign) _____

Mail to the **Reader Service:**
IN U.S.A.: P.O. Box 1867, Buffalo, NY 14240-1867
IN CANADA: P.O. Box 609, Fort Erie, Ontario L2A 5X3

Want to try two free books from another line?
Call 1-800-873-8635 or visit www.ReaderService.com.

* Terms and prices subject to change without notice. Prices do not include applicable taxes. Sales tax applicable in N.Y. Canadian residents will be charged applicable taxes. Offer not valid in Quebec. This offer is limited to one order per household. Not valid for current subscribers to Harlequin Western Romance books. All orders subject to credit approval. Credit or debit balances in a customer's account(s) may be offset by any other outstanding balance owed by or to the customer. Please allow 4 to 6 weeks for delivery. Offer available while quantities last.

Your Privacy—The Reader Service is committed to protecting your privacy. Our Privacy Policy is available online at www.ReaderService.com or upon request from the Reader Service.

We make a portion of our mailing list available to reputable third parties that offer products we believe may interest you. If you prefer that we not exchange your name with third parties, or if you wish to clarify or modify your communication preferences, please visit us at www.ReaderService.com/consumerschoice or write to us at Reader Service Preference Service, P.O. Box 9062, Buffalo, NY 14240-9062. Include your complete name and address.

HWR16

READERSERVICE.COM

Manage your account online!

- Review your order history
- Manage your payments
- Update your address

*We've designed the
Reader Service website
just for you.*

Enjoy all the features!

- Discover new series available to you, and read excerpts from any series.
- Respond to mailings and special monthly offers.
- Connect with favorite authors at the blog.
- Browse the Bonus Bucks catalog and online-only exculsives.
- Share your feedback.

Visit us at:
ReaderService.com

RS15